To my … harlie
Ge…

CW01594164

With love,
R

A Christmas Spirit

by

Rikki

authorHOUSE™
1663 Liberty Drive, Suite 200
Bloomington, Indiana 47403
(800) 839-8640
www.AuthorHouse.com

This book is a work of fiction. People, places, events, and situations are the product of the author's imagination. Any resemblance to actual persons, living or dead, or historical events, is purely coincidental.

First published by AuthorHouse 09/22/05

ISBN: 1-4208-8548-0 (sc)

Printed in the United States of America
Bloomington, Indiana

This book is printed on acid-free paper.

This book is dedicated to my very dear friend, Kathy Baxter, in Calgary, Alberta, whom I love and admire very much, and who is a source of hope and inspiration to me every day.

One

It should have been the most happy and exciting time of the year. But as she trudged through the drifting snow in the darkness of the late winter afternoon, Kathy Lane was angered by the twinkling coloured lights, the garlands and the wreaths which seemed only to mock her. With her gloved hand holding her tiny daughter's mittened one a little tighter, the distraught mother fought back waves of tears. As the two made their way along the crowded sidewalk, the happy chatter of passing shoppers slammed into her like a physical assault.

The doctor had just delivered the news that this family had been dreading in the few years since the little girl's birth. Kathy's thoughts drifted back to that day, as easily and as gently as the soft snowflakes fell around her. After she and her husband, Robert, had been given two beautiful sons, James and Elijah, the new parents were thrilled at the arrival of their sweet girl, who made their family complete.

Their joy soon turned to terror when moments after her birth, there was a flurry of activity around the tiny baby. The doctor and nurses spoke in hushed tones, working quickly as they huddled around the girl, and the atmosphere sent an icy chill through her frightened parents.

Suddenly, the wee babe was whisked off to the Neonatal Intensive Care Unit (NICU) while someone mumbled something about further tests. One nurse remained, tending to paperwork and sorting out instruments, while another tended to Kathy, trying to calm the terrified mother.

The baby having been rushed away to the NICU, the doctor turned her attention back to Kathy, working quickly and quietly. Robert, a doctor himself, tried to probe the obstetrician for answers, but the only reply she would give was that her area of expertise was women's medicine, and the baby needed a paediatrician to be sure she was all right.

Kathy dissolved into tears as Robert stood dumbfounded for a few moments before he could collect himself and console his exhausted, weeping wife. Holding her while she sobbed, he thought about how long they had wanted this little girl, how precious she was to her parents. When Kathy was seven months pregnant with Elijah, she had been in a terrible car accident, sustaining life-threatening injuries. Defying the odds, she survived, but during the emergency Caesarean section to deliver her son, the doctors found that there had been extensive internal damage, and she was told that she would be unable to bear any more children.

She and Robert were stunned. They had planned on a large family, with lots of sons and daughters, and it was a blow for which the young couple was unprepared.

But Kathy was a fighter. She had a long period of rehabilitation and physiotherapy to get through, and she was determined to regain her former level of health and abilities. The doctors did not know just how driven she could be, and she was not about to let them tell her whether or not she would once again experience the joy of bringing a new life into the world.

As the years passed, Kathy and Robert were elated, but then increasingly heartbroken when their love for each other resulted in many pregnancies, all of which ended tragically in miscarriages.

There came a time when once again, Kathy felt the first waves of morning sickness, and after so many shattering disappointments, she dared not even hope that she was, indeed, expecting another baby. Before long, however, there was no doubt. The doctor's tone was almost reluctant, her eyes filled with anticipatory sympathy, as she gave Kathy the news that there was yet another little life growing inside her body.

The expectant mother was certain that this time would be different, and she pushed aside the look and the tone, adamantly insisting that this child would be born, healthy and strong. Ignoring the doctor's knowing expression, she mumbled a quick thank you, and left the office, countless emotions rolling through her, each one coming on top of the last, faster than she could even identify them.

Of course, there was the joy and elation at the prospect of motherhood again, mixed with great fear and worry, wondering when she might lose this tiny little person. But something felt different; it was as though her baby was speaking to her, its little spirit crying out, telling its mother not to worry, that her dreams would be fulfilled if she would just believe.

Elijah was a particularly spiritual child, and had come to believe that everything happened for a reason. Still, he mourned with his family each time their dream shattered. Then came the day that his parents announced that there was yet another baby trying to make its way into the world. He knew this one would be different; he was certain that he was going to meet this little person. Though he'd have had trouble putting it into words, had he been asked, he felt a connection to the tiny baby who was growing inside his mother. Certain it was a girl, he felt as though she was speaking to him, letting him know that she was on her way, and that she wanted him to be her big brother. And he was happy to answer her, sending messages that he was honoured to have been given the job.

Because of his peaceful, spiritual nature, Kathy and Robert tended to forget that Elijah was still just a child. He was so sweet and easy to be around, never gave them a moment's worry; I suppose to some extent, it was easy for him to be forgotten by his parents. Of course, they loved him dearly, and he knew that. He did not need much from them; however, his old soul sometimes made it hard for them to see the little boy of 10 who still needed hugs and cuddles. He refused to let this bother him, content in the knowledge that he was loved.

James had a little more trouble with being positive after so many disappointments. He was a quiet and introverted young man of 15, who felt things very deeply, and on the subject of another baby, he was rather conflicted. Though he wanted his parents to experience the joy of having the child they so desperately wanted, his protective nature also made him feel somewhat resentful of each tiny person who ended up causing them so much pain. It had got to the point that he even resented the Dream Child that they wanted; it seemed that his parents spent increasing amounts of time and energy on their preoccupation with a baby that may never exist. He longed for the way things used to be, when he, his brother and their parents just enjoyed being together as they were. But for years, the Dream Child had taken centre stage, and as far as James could see, it was chipping away at every relationship in the family, even though he was certain he was the only one who noticed.

Robert fiercely loved his wife and their sons. As a doctor, he witnessed many terrible and painful aspects of life, and this perspective allowed him to value his family in a way that he could not describe. He had been driving the car when it was broadsided during an icy storm, his wife's door taking the full impact of the other vehicle. Guilt-ridden, he blamed himself, although no charges were laid because of the weather conditions. It was truly an accident, or so said the police report. Yet Robert was plagued with 'If onlys', believing that it was his fault for years afterward.

It was bad enough that he felt responsible for the accident, but the resulting issue of childbearing problems weighed heavily on his conscience. Although there was no legitimate reason for him to blame himself, Robert felt as though he had been the cause of his wife's horrific injuries and long recovery, and he believed that he had taken away her lifelong desire for many children.

Over the years, he had retreated into himself, feeling as though he was the reason for much of the family's heartbreak and hardship. Being a doctor only amplified his struggles; he believed he should have been able to do more for his wife after the accident. In his head, he realized that it was impossible. But in his heart -- well, that was another story.

Knowing how much his wife wanted more children, he was only too happy to try to make her dream come true. And if they were lucky enough to have even one more child, he believed it would also wipe the slate clean, relieving him of his guilt, his burden. He, too, adored children, and it was easy for him to be excited about the idea of creating another baby with the woman he loved. But with each tragic miscarriage, his guilt about the accident and his feelings of inadequacy as a doctor only deepened, and his desire to relieve both only grew.

Although this was a family of people who loved each other very deeply, it was also fractured, even if none of its members seemed to notice -- or maybe they simply wouldn't acknowledge it, because to do so -- well, the stakes were very high.

And on this bustling, snowy street, with strains of cheery Christmas carols taunting her as they were piped outside from many of the shops, Kathy was overwhelmed with the realization that the fracture was about to become a major break.

It was a short walk from the doctor's surgery to the car. Kathy knew that her beloved Angelina was too ill to walk any great distance, and had done her best to park nearby. After securing the little girl in her car seat, Kathy got in behind the wheel and slammed the door. Instantly, the rest of the world was blocked out, and the silence was deafening. The crowds of people and the music had been a bit of a distraction, but sitting in the car, just the two of them as they had done countless times before, there was no more escaping reality.

The car keys still in her hand, Kathy sat still and quiet as the doctor's words resounded in her head, spinning and swirling faster and faster, until she thought she would scream. It seemed that she had been sitting there for an eternity, though it was really only a minute or two. Just as Kathy was certain she was about to fly apart, Angelina's sweet voice broke through the exploding words in her mother's head.

"Look, Mama! A little angel, just like me!"

Kathy's blood ran cold, the child's nickname ringing in her ears like never before. Recalling the miracle of the little girl's birth and that her name had been chosen because she was truly Heaven sent, Kathy was horrified to think that "Little Angel" may soon have an entirely different meaning.

Pulling herself together for the child's sake, she looked in the rear view mirror, and saw that as she pointed, Angelina's beautiful and delicate face was alive with excitement, despite the obvious appearance of ill health. Following the direction of her daughter's tiny hand, Kathy saw an angel in the window of a shop. Wearing a white dress with gold embroidery, the angel decoration appeared to be a child with feathery white wings, rosy cheeks, blonde curls and wide, innocent eyes. Apart from Angelina's dark hair, the resemblance between her and the decoration sent an icy chill up Kathy's spine. Although the child had never been very well, there had been times when she had had some colour in her beautiful face. And upon seeing the rosy complexion on this little angel, Kathy could not help but see her own sweet child and realize that she would never look well again.

"See, Mama? It looks just like me, and I'm your Little Angel! Except my hair isn't yellow!"

It was all Kathy could do not to bite right through her lip as she choked back the sobs that she knew were desperate to escape. It took everything she had to force a smile on her face as she replied, "Yes, my darling. It looks just like you. Except your hair isn't yellow."

With one long and thoughtful look at her sweet daughter, Kathy inserted the key into the ignition, started the car, and began the journey home, winding their way through the rolling hills and the little lanes of Northern England as the delicate snowflakes continued to fall.

When the two had finally pulled up in front of their cottage, Kathy was surprised to find that she had actually managed to get them there safely. She did not remember the drive at all, so preoccupied was she. Knowing that she had to share the news with Robert, who was not yet home from work, she wrestled with when and how to tell him.

A forced smile on her lips, she lifted the child out of the car, and put her on the drive. Turning to close the car door, she paused, closing her eyes to absorb the sound of crunching snow under Angelina's boots, desperate to hang onto every single moment of the little girl's life.

Once inside, Kathy sent Angelina to find her brothers, suggesting that she ask them to play one of her favourite movies for her. As the little girl disappeared up the stairs, calling her brothers by name, Kathy headed for the sitting room, lit a fire and poured a rather stiff shot of whisky before sinking into a chair.

Alone at last, the tears welled up in her eyes as she stared at the flickering flames, though she did not see them. Rather, she was recalling memories of Angelina, reliving the joy that her beautiful daughter had shared with all who knew her. In her mind's eye, there was Angelina, running and dancing in the garden, peals of her infectious laughter ringing out, delighting all who heard it. She saw the little girl, sleeping peacefully, her beloved Teddy tucked under one arm, a few loose curls splayed across her forehead. The heartbroken mother recalled each of Angelina's few birthday parties, the tiny tot's eyes sparkling with excitement, opening gifts, or blowing our candles on a cake. Memory after memory rolled through Kathy's mind, like a film about Angelina's life.

Deep in thought, and entirely on edge, Kathy jumped when Robert suddenly appeared at her side, and affectionately stroked her hair. She had not heard him come in, and was not yet prepared to share the horrible news. But there was no more time to consider what she should say.

Leaning over and kissing his wife gently on her cheek as she turned her face upward, he could see by her expression and her tears that he need not ask the question. Still, he had to speak.

"I'm so sorry I couldn't get to the appointment, but I had to do an emergency surgery which shouldn't have taken long. We ran into some complications and I simply couldn't get away. I hope you got the message I left with the doctor's office."

"Yes, I did." Kathy's throat strained to get the words past the lump that was choking her. "I was sorry to hear that you couldn't be there. I know, it was beyond your control. But if ever there was a day I needed you..." Her voice trailed off as she stared into the fire and let the silence speak for her.

His body taut, Robert felt the blood drain from his head. His heart began to beat wildly in his chest, and he could feel it pounding, his breath coming quicker as adrenalin began to flood through him. Swearing his veins were suddenly filled with ice water, Robert was afraid to say a word. As long as he did not speak, they could go on for just a few more minutes or hours, or maybe months or years, thinking Angelina would be all right. He knew that once he spoke again, Kathy's answer would shatter their lives into a million pieces. Still, he could not help hanging onto the present, savouring the last few seconds before their world changed forever.

He stood unmoving for several moments, trying to figure out what he should say. Finally, he opened his mouth and some words came out, with no real thought behind them, since he could find no way to ask the question in a way that didn't repulse him beyond description.

"Is it as bad as we think?" was his simple, yet not-so-simple question.

Kathy's eyes filled with tears again, and the aching lump in her throat was almost more than she could bear. "Yes," came the stiff reply. "He said the latest test results are extremely disturbing, and as we knew would happen someday, it seems that we are nearing the end." Kathy's voice began to break, and she needed a moment before she could continue.

For years, Robert had been anticipating this moment, wondering exactly when and how it would occur, imagining how it might feel. And now he had his answer, yet there was no way to describe the shock and the horror of hearing that they were very likely a short time away from watching their darling daughter die. His mind was racing with questions and thoughts; he could not finish one before another crowded round it, and another, and another. Would they tell

Angelina? When would they tell the boys? Would it be quick for Angelina? Or would she have to suffer?

Between the thoughts that were flooding his mind, and the feelings which overwhelmed him, Robert was reeling. Suddenly becoming light-headed, he sank into the nearest chair, pale, and trembling on the inside.

After a few deep breaths, Kathy spoke once again. "He said it looks like it could be very soon, although there is faintest hope that she will manage to recover somewhat and give us more time with her. He reminded me that she's been quite ill before, yet she surprised everyone with more of an improvement than was expected. However, this time...well, she's never had test results like this before."

At that, she finally broke down completely. Robert, being a doctor, had witnessed the recent changes in Angelina and was not surprised by the news, but the father in him was entirely unprepared to hear the words that told him that his sweet little girl, not yet five years old, may well die before long. He helped Kathy to get up from the chair, and the parents, hearts breaking, held each other for a long time.

Two

It had been a week since the family got The News. Kathy and Robert had decided it was best to prepare the boys, despite the fact that it was the Christmas season. Although they hoped that Angelina would once again improve, the odds were not in her favour. It seemed only fair that the boys should be allowed to make the most of what was likely to be the last part of her very short life.

Elijah had taken the news as well as any 10-year-old boy could be expected to do, and that was only because of his intensely spiritual nature. He knew in his heart that if she was not meant to be with them, then there must be a reason, a higher purpose, and they must accept it as such. However, he was still just a boy, and he loved his little sister very deeply. He had always taken such an interest in her, enjoying playing games with her and making up little plays and magic shows for the family. He would be the magician, and she would be his assistant. They spent countless hours together, using their imaginations and having a wonderful time.

Outwardly, James seemed to take the news well. No strong reactions, no display of emotion. But inside, he felt as though a sword had pierced his heart. This was far beyond anything he could have imagined. This was worse than his mother's car accident and all the miscarriages combined.

His pain soon turned to rage as he wondered why on earth the family, and especially poor, sweet Angelina, had to endure such suffering. Unable to understand a spiritual perspective on this and other tragedies, he had turned further away from any sense of the Divine each time the family experienced a traumatic event. He could not believe in any kind of God or Higher Power that would cause so much pain.

Swallowing his anger, it fed on itself, though no one was aware of what was going on inside the very sensitive boy. He loved his little sister; she had always been such a source of light and joy in the family, and more particularly, in his life. Often, she would take her dolls or toys into his room, and play quietly on his bed while he sat and played his guitar. She loved his music, and felt very important because her oldest brother allowed her to listen to him practice, even sharing with her the songs he was writing, and asking for her opinions.

James also loved to read, and he enjoyed sharing his love of books with her. It was not an uncommon sight to find the two of them curled up together, Angelina usually on his lap, snuggled against his chest, while he read her favourite stories over and over, although to her, each time might as well have been the first, so intent was she on every word and every picture.

Living just outside a village as they did, they were surrounded by meadows with many wooded areas. A little creek bubbled and trickled as it wound its way through the trees. When the weather was suitable, the two would often take their books, and sometimes a little snack, and they would go and sit by the water for ages. On many occasions, Angelina fell asleep and had a little nap, curled up against James, his arm around her while he read to himself. Being with this adorable child was the closest he came to experiencing any spiritual feelings; he loved to listen to her deep, even breathing, and her little girl squeaks and sighs when she stretched in her sleep, while she snuggled in a little closer.

And in those quiet, private moments, James allowed himself to consider the notion that there was more to life than just the human experience.

The first thing on the morning after Angelina's appointment, Robert had called her doctor for more details. Of course, Kathy had related all she had been told, but he needed to hear every aspect of the test results. Desperately hoping that Kathy had been so emotional that she had misinterpreted and overstated the doctor's words, he prayed for better news. The two physicians went over every one of Angelina's tests, and sadly, Robert learned that Kathy had been right. Yes, there was always the possibility that somehow, the child would surprise them and improve, at least for a while, but it seemed highly unlikely. The best they could do was hope and pray -- and prepare themselves for the worst.

Kathy had spent the week struggling to keep from sliding into a major depression, choking back floods of tears. The only thing that kept her from falling into a deep pit of despair was the knowledge that her family, and especially her Little Angel, needed her. With Christmas approaching, there was plenty to do to keep her busy. Angelina had always loved Christmas, of course, and being the youngest, it was an even more magical time for her than for the rest of her family.

But little did she know that it meant far more to them each year than she could imagine, because they had always been well aware that each one could be her last.

Christmas is an emotional season at the best of times, but this particular one had the family on a roller coaster. It would have been easy for everyone to allow the heavy, black cloud to descend upon them entirely, yet they were determined to make this the best holiday they had ever had.

This desire was driven by their love for their Little Angel; it was she who inspired them to truly appreciate every moment, and to dive into the shopping, wrapping, baking and excitement of the season. Christmas music filled the house, as preparations were made for the upcoming holiday. Although Angelina seemed to grow a little weaker and a little more pale each day, her presence kept the magic alive. Everyone was found singing or humming Christmas carols on occasion; everyone, that is, except James. It just was not in his nature.

One Friday evening a couple of weeks before Christmas, as Kathy and Robert were tucking Angelina into bed, the little girl looked up at her parents and asked, "When am I going to go and see Father Christmas?"

Kathy looked questioningly at Robert; both parents were wondering whether the ailing child could withstand such a long outing.

"Well," Robert replied, "Mummy and I will discuss it. Are you sure you feel well enough? You know you will probably have to wait in a queue for a very long time, and you tire so easily because you haven't been feeling very well."

"Oh, yes, Daddy!" was the eager reply. "I can sit in my stroller and have a little nap if I get tired! I'll be all right! Please? Please may I see Father Christmas? I have to tell him what I want or he might not know!"

The two parents could not help but smile at each other, and at their sweet and innocent little girl. Scooping her into a warm embrace as she lay in her bed, Robert said, "Of course, Little Angel. We will take you to see Father Christmas. How about first thing tomorrow? If we go early enough, maybe we can avoid having to wait for a really long time."

"Oh, goodie!!" cried Angelina, as she squeezed her father a little tighter. "Thank you, Daddy!"

And with goodnight hugs and kisses all around, Teddy tucked in with his charge, the bedside lamp was turned off and Angelina was left to go to sleep, with Frank, the kitten she had got for her last birthday, curled up at her feet.

The morning brought with it bright sunshine, which made the frost and snow sparkle like millions of tiny diamonds. Kathy was awake very early, hours before the sun rose. Creeping out of her bed, she wrapped her dressing gown tightly around her as she made her way to the kitchen in the darkness. It was becoming increasingly difficult for her to sleep more than a few restless hours each night, as she watched her beloved Angelina grow more weak and pale each day. She clung to the faintest hope that the little girl would rally, and would begin to feel a little better, and give the family more time with her, but each morning, one look at the child made Kathy's heart sink a little further.

Snapping on a light in the kitchen, Kathy headed for the fridge to take out the coffee grounds. Reaching for the handle, she stopped and stared at the artwork hanging next to it on the door. Angelina had made a picture of a Christmas tree, with colourful decorations on it, and a little angel on top. There were bright packages under the tree, and all her family stood around, stick people with huge smiles on all the faces. In four-year-old style, everything was coloured outside the lines that she had drawn, but there was no mistaking the radiant, cheerful, little girl energy in the picture. Kathy felt an ache in her heart that defied description. She froze, staring at the picture for several moments, struggling to choke back waves of sobs, a common occurrence since that horrible appointment with the doctor.

Finally, she collected herself and managed to make a pot of coffee, then sank into a chair at the table, trying not to look at the picture. Wherever she looked, she could feel it, as if it were staring at her, calling to her, drawing her to it. She could not help but find herself once again contemplating when and how Angelina would die. Would it be at home? Would it be in the hospital? Would she be alone, or would anyone in the family be with her? And how would she and Robert plan, never mind get through her funeral? These questions had been gnawing at her since they had received the terrible news, and with each passing day, the likelihood of finding the answers grew.

Kathy rose and poured a cup of coffee, then padded into the sitting room and lit a fire. It would be another couple of hours until daylight, and this was a good time to write in her journal. She had always kept one, though it had been sporadic due to the 'busyness' of life. But lately, she had written frequently, sometimes a few times a day, wanting to record every bit of

Angelina's life. She did not want to forget any tiny part of it; she wanted to be able to relive it, if...

Turning on a small lamp next to the old wing-back chair by the fireplace, Kathy sat down with her book and pen. The time flew, as she thought about anything and everything she wanted to say since her last writing, the day before. Occasionally, she got up to stoke the fire, add another log, or refill her cup with coffee.

Just as the sun was beginning to peek over the horizon, casting a soft and rosy glow, Kathy heard quiet little footsteps coming down the stairs behind her. Looking over her shoulder, she saw her sleepy daughter, clutching Teddy and rubbing one eye with her little knuckles.

"Is it time to see Father Christmas yet?" were the first words out of Angelina's mouth, as she climbed onto her mother's lap and snuggled into the early morning hug.

Kathy could not help but smile, and chuckled softly as she said, "No, sweetheart, he's still sleeping. He works very late every night these days, but he'll be up soon and will be ready to go to the mall to see you and the other children today. Are you sure you feel well enough to go?"

"Oh, yes, Mama! I'm so excited!" replied Angelina, with a pleading expression as she looked up at her mother.

Kathy looked down at her daughter, tousled dark curls framing her pale but still beautiful face. "Alright, if you're sure." But Kathy, afraid that too much excitement or activity might shorten the child's remaining time, would have preferred to keep Angelina home and quiet. She was torn, knowing that she wanted her daughter to live her life to the fullest, but desperately wanting to protect her, to keep her alive.

"I have an idea, my darling. How would you like to help me make some muffins for breakfast?" Kathy asked.

Angelina needed no encouragement, since she loved to bake. Climbing down from Kathy's lap, she was already in the kitchen before her mother got out of the chair.

Robert had been lying awake for a while, not at all surprised to find that he had awakened alone once again. As the morning light crept softly into the room, his heart was heavy, knowing that he could not relieve his wife of her burden, nor his children of theirs.

He knew, too, that they were looking to him to be strong, to carry them through the coming days. What he did not know was how he would get through them himself. He only hoped that in being a source of strength for them, he would be able to cope with his own tremendous guilt and grief.

A hint of cinnamon and coffee wafted into the room and soon got his attention, bringing him back to the present. Weary from yet another poor night's sleep filled with disturbing dreams, he swung his legs out of the bed and put his feet on the floor. Sitting for a few moments, his elbows resting on his thighs, he tried to gather his thoughts, preparing to face another day. He headed for the shower, hoping it would refresh him somewhat, and allow him to put on a cheerful front.

By the time he found himself walking into the kitchen, sunlight was streaming through the windows. Kathy and Elijah were laying the table for breakfast, and Angelina was seeing to food and fresh water for Frank. James was nowhere in sight, typical for the teen on a weekend morning. It seemed such a normal day, and for a brief moment, Robert could pretend that they were like any other family, without the black, oppressive cloud that hung over them.

"Daddy!" squealed Angelina, as she ran to him for a hug and a good morning kiss. "I get to see Father Christmas today!"

"Yes, Angel, you do!" he smiled.

"I helped Mummy make breakfast! See? We made muffins and bacon, and we're going to have eggs, too, as soon as James comes down!" The little girl was beaming, yet her illness was still clearly visible on her face.

"I'll go and see if I can rouse him," said Robert, as he turned and headed for the boy's room.

The door was closed, as usual. Knocking softly, Robert called the boy's name a few times before getting a mumbled reply. Slowly opening the door, Robert entered the darkened room. "Come on, James. It's time to get up. Breakfast is waiting and we must take Angelina to see Father Christmas first thing so she doesn't have to wait in the queue too long."

There was no reply.

"James?" queried Robert. "Did you hear me?"

"Yeah, I heard you." The boy sounded angry.

More silence.

"Are you coming down then?" Robert was unwilling to explore James's feelings at that moment; coping with his own was difficult enough.

"Yeah, I'm coming." Again, an angry tone.

Robert left the room, closing the door behind him. He had never been particularly good at reaching James, or knowing what went on inside his son, and he was certain that it was going to get a whole lot worse. He could not deal with that now; he had to just get through each day, one at a time. And he returned to the kitchen.

Elijah was helping Kathy with the eggs, and Angelina was sitting on the floor, petting Frank, who was purring happily in her 'Mummy's' arms. Robert finished getting things on the table, filling his and Kathy's cups with fresh coffee, and putting a glass of juice at each place. Just as the four were seating themselves, James stumbled into the kitchen, looking sullen and sleepy in his bathrobe. Instantly, the energy in the room changed, his moodiness seeming to affect everyone. Well, everyone except Angelina, that is, who delighted in seeing her oldest brother appear, whatever his mood.

"Good morning, James!" the little girl bubbled as she leaned over and hugged one side of him as he took his place next to her at the table.

Immediately, his expression softened and he smiled as he said, "Good morning, Sweetpea" and kissed her on the top of her head. Although he seemed far from happy, at least the cloud had lifted somewhat, and the family managed to enjoy their breakfast together.

Robert and Elijah did the washing up when they were finished, while Kathy helped Angelina dress and fix her hair. She headed for the shower and got herself ready to go, while James was off doing the same. Just before the mall opened, the family was ready and on the way for Angelina's big day.

Arriving at 'The North Pole' in the shopping centre, they were happy to see that although there was a queue, it was not terribly long. Taking their place, they began their wait, her parents and brothers delighting in the excitement on Angelina's face. She was quieter than in previous Father Christmas visits, but there was no mistaking the sparkle in her eyes. It was a look that they all believed they would never forget. Robert had been sure to bring the video camera, and James was happy to do the recording. He panned 'The North Pole', and a few other children sitting on Father Christmas's knee, and was sure to get plenty of shots of Angelina, being a little ham for the camera as she sat in her stroller, showing remarkable patience for an excited four-year-old.

As the people ahead of them moved up, one by one, it was easy to see that the little girl was tiring, though her excitement never waned. Finally, it was her turn. Robert lifted her out of the stroller and she made her way up to the large man in the red suit, eagerly climbing onto his lap.

"Happy Christmas! And what is your name, little girl?" he asked.

"I'm Angelina, Father Christmas!" was her smiling reply.

"Have you been a good girl this year?" was the next, and expected question.

"Well, I've tried very hard, Father Christmas, but sometimes, I know I've annoyed my big brothers when I didn't mean to. Does that count?" Her little face wore a concerned expression.

Father Christmas's reply was a big belly laugh, as he told her that's what little girls were meant to do, and he told her he was sure that she had been very good.

"Oh, I'm so glad, because what I want is very, very important and I would be very sad if I can't have it!"

It was Father Christmas's turn to look concerned, and with feigned seriousness as he asked, "Oh? And what might that be, young lady?"

"Well, my family has been really sad for a while because I'm very sick, and I really want them to be happy again. Please, Father Christmas, can you make them be happy?"

The man was dumbfounded. He had heard stories like this, and had seen it in the movies, but could not believe that there really were such children on this earth. He did not know how to reply; of course, this was something he could not fix. In his shock, he could not answer for a moment, but finally replied. "I'm sure your family loves you very much, Angelina, and if you don't feel well, of course they will be sad. But once you're better, they will be happy."

"But I don't think I'm going to get better, Father Christmas. No one says it to me, but I just feel it."

Once again, the man was stunned and silent. He had never been faced with such a situation, and had no idea how to respond. He decided that rather than address this issue, he would ask, "Well, Angelina, I hope you do get better soon. But can you tell me if there's something I can get for you for Christmas, like a toy or a doll?"

Angelina had to think for a minute. She had come to him with only her other request on her mind, but finally said that she would really love a Raggedy Ann.

Father Christmas said that he was sure he could manage that, and after wishing her a happy holiday, he looked over at her family, standing a few feet away. The expressions on their faces spoke volumes, and he knew that Angelina's situation was, indeed, very serious. As he gave them a sympathetic look, Angelina returned to her stroller. Kathy and Robert did not smile as they looked back at him, and watched as the next excited little child climbed up onto his lap.

The visit with Father Christmas over, and having heard what Angelina had said to him, Kathy and Robert looked at each other, wanting to discuss it, but knowing this was not the time.

The trip had worn out the ailing child, so rather than window shop, the family headed for home.

Three

After returning from the visit to Father Christmas, Angelina had gone to bed for a nap. The other four members of her family gathered at the kitchen table to talk about what she had said on the old man's lap. They had fooled themselves into believing that Angelina was unaware of how ill she was, but they realized that they had been very wrong.

Though each of the family members was dealing with Angelina's illness in his or her own way, there was one important common feeling which led to a unanimous decision: This family had to do anything and everything possible to put on happier faces for Angelina, and to give her a sense of peace, so she would know that they were going to be all right.

And in the days since they had that conversation, the mood in the house had been considerably lighter. No, it was not a jolly home, by any means. But everyone focused on making it as happy a home as they could for the little girl as Christmas rapidly approached. Uppermost in their minds was what she had said to Father Christmas, and her words brought each of the other family members out of his or her own feelings, reminding all of them that there was something else more important.

The family was most surprised when they found that they could be happy again, even though it was a very bittersweet time. Angelina's visit with Father Christmas had allowed them to feel a little excited about the holiday again. With renewed enthusiasm, they were only too happy to dive into baking shortbread stars, angels and Christmas trees, or filling the house with the warm and wonderful aroma of spicy Gingerbread men, which Angelina and the boys would happily decorate together. It was obvious that Angelina's health was failing quickly, and she was unable to do very much at once, frequently needing to lie down and rest. But even then, she was surrounded by family, as they took turns reading to her, or singing Christmas carols as she drifted off to sleep.

About a week before Christmas, Robert came in on a Friday evening, dragging a big, beautiful tree behind him. The children were excited when they saw it, and even James could not help but smile as he hurried with Elijah to the cellar to find the boxes of lights and decorations. As Robert hauled the tree into the sitting room and secured it in its stand, Kathy stoked the fire and put on a CD of Christmas carols. Retreating into the kitchen, she made a huge pot of steaming hot chocolate, and arranged a plate of goodies that the family had been baking in recent days.

Angelina smiled weakly from the settee as she watched everyone bustling around, getting ready to decorate the tree and the house. She was thrilled to see everyone so much happier, and with Frank curled up and sleeping on her chest, she felt peaceful for the first time in ages.

Each time the boys came up from the cellar, there were more boxes of decorations to open. They were placed on the floor next to her so she could get a good look at them, and feel as though she was helping by handing them to her family as they hung garlands and set little ornaments here and there. Once in a while, she disturbed Frank, rising from the settee and choosing a few decorations for the tree, putting them on the lower boughs, which were the only ones that she could reach. She especially loved the Victorian ornaments; little rocking horses, pretty quilted, lace-trimmed stars and bows, wooden soldiers and a little red and green grandfather clock, among others.

A beautiful wreath was hung on the front door, and some reindeer with Father Christmas in his sleigh were stood on the porch. As everyone sipped on hot chocolate and nibbled on cookies and squares, they found themselves to be the happiest they had been in a very long time. Singing along to the Christmas carols, there was a warmth and a closeness that had been missing for some time, as each member of the family had been lost in his or her own pain.

And finally came the moment for which they had all been waiting. From amongst the boxes of decorations, James pulled out a basket which contained something wrapped in several layers of tissue. He knew that he had to be very careful with it, and as he peeled back each piece of tissue, the family was silent. Gingerly, he removed what was inside: a beautiful, porcelain angel for the top of the tree. It had been in Kathy's family for many generations, and for being well over 100 years old, it was in perfect condition, except for a tiny chip on the left wing.

Tradition dictated that the youngest child present and able was meant to secure the angel to the top of the Christmas tree, and make a wish. And it was said that if the angel broke, something very bad would happen. No one knew how the story began; they only knew of its existence. Because of its age and the story, the angel was always handled with the utmost care, and on this occasion, it was no different.

"Angelina," said Robert, "are you able to put the angel on the tree?"

The little girl was quiet for a moment, weighing how she was feeling physically against her desire to do her duty as the youngest child present. Finally, she spoke, and in a very solemn tone, she said, "Yes, Daddy. I can do it."

Everyone smiled, wanting her to be the one to fulfill this task; it seemed even more important than ever. The previous year, she had been too little to be able to manage it at three years old, so this was to be her first time. And, the family feared, her last. Robert showed her the clips on the angel, and explained how it attached to the top of the tree. When she was certain that she understood, he lifted the little girl, who was hugging the angel tightly against her chest.

The room was lit only by the fire, the lights on the trees, and many candles. "Silent Night" was playing on the stereo as Robert lifted the girl so that she could reach the top of the tree. Taking her responsibility very seriously, Angelina carefully secured the angel in its place of honour.

"Make a wish, Angel! Make a wish!" cried Elijah, excited about his sister's success.

Angelina closed her eyes, and with "Silent Night" still playing in the dimly lit room, her sweet little voice echoed the sentiments of everyone present.

"I wish I could live to see another Christmas."

Robert, Kathy and the boys were stunned. No one could find any words, but all eyes were filled with tears, while the CD went into "O Holy Night". Everyone stood in silence, Robert still holding Angelina, and all eyes were upon her, when suddenly, the unthinkable happened. The angel fell from the tree and smashed.

Poor Angelina! She burst into tears, and buried her face in her father's chest. Attempting to console her with hugs and kisses, he told her not to worry, it was just an ornament. No one knew what to say, and although none of them wanted to admit to it, they were all feeling rather superstitious right at that moment. They wondered if, indeed, there was any truth to the story which had been handed down for generations.

"Oh, Daddy! I broke the angel! It was so old and so special, and I ruined it!" And the little girl burst into a new wave of sobs.

"It's okay, Angel, it's just an ornament," Robert said, trying to reassure the child that it was really not important.

"No, it's not okay! So many other Christmases and no one broke it! I'm so sorry! And what if it's true, Daddy? What if something bad happens now because of that?" The poor child was inconsolable.

"Angelina, it's an ornament. It's just a story that people made up about it, probably because little children were meant to attach it to the tree, and telling them such a story would make them be very careful. Ornaments don't have power like that. Please don't worry." Robert was unsuccessfully trying to calm the little girl, who would simply not stop crying.

Kathy bent down to pick up the pieces of the angel, while Elijah ran for a broom and dustpan. James retreated to his room, unable to cope with the reason for Angelina's wish. The little girl cried for some time, though Elijah and her parents tried everything possible to cheer her and take her mind off the incident, to no avail.

At last, Angelina stopped sobbing, and Robert settled her into a big chair with a blanket and Frank. Elijah got one of her favourite books and began to read to her, and eventually, the little girl nodded off.

Robert picked up the sleeping child and carried her to her bed. Tucking her in, and kissing her goodnight, he fought back waves of tears, recalling her wish, and lay with her for a long time in her room, lit only by the dim hall light.

Kathy and Elijah tidied up the boxes from decorating and washed the dishes from the family's snack of hot chocolate and cookies, then sat together at the kitchen table to play cards. Both wanted to speak with James and Robert, though they did not discuss it. They were well aware that it was best to leave them alone for the time being, though it tugged at their hearts to leave the two in so much pain.

When Robert finally emerged from Angelina's room and returned to the sitting room, the fire had been reduced to glowing embers. The CD had long since stopped playing, and the house was very quiet, except for the soft voices of his wife and youngest son in the kitchen. Feeling as though he needed to be alone, he headed upstairs for bed without a word to them.

James had spent the duration of the evening playing his guitar, crying while he did so, his heart breaking for his little sister, desperately wishing he could make this all go away. He hoped that no one would come to his door; he did not want anyone to see him in tears. While he played, he kept looking at his bed, envisioning little Angelina there with her dolls and her toys, wide-eyed and thrilled to be with her big brother. And with each of these images, James wept even harder.

Finally, he could stand it no longer, and he crawled into his bed, turned out the light beside it, and cried until he fell into a fitful sleep.

By morning, Angelina's parents and brothers had managed to regain their composure and were once again able to focus on the request the child had made when she saw Father Christmas. They did their best to be cheerful, but it was clear that Angelina had taken a turn for the worse. The house was very quiet on that cloudy, cold Saturday morning, until Elijah thought that maybe a magic show was just what they needed.

Angelina was too ill to be his assistant that day, but he managed to put on an entertaining performance for the rest of his family. He had a lovely sense of humour, and he was in rare form that day. Even Angelina, as sick as she was, laughed out loud a few times, which warmed the hearts of everyone present.

As it turned out, Elijah's magic did the trick, and it seemed to pull everyone out of the slump they had been in that day.

After dinner, some families from the village came by for a visit, and the Lane family had a sort of impromptu party. Angelina was not up to a lot of conversation, but she did enjoy seeing everyone from her 'bed' on the settee. The tree was beautiful, even without the angel on top, and the house was filled with the warmth of loving family and friends. The little girl sat back and took it all in, with Frank sleeping on her chest for most of the evening.

The guests had brought Christmas gifts and put them under the tree. They also came with plates of home-baked biscuits and squares, and everyone had a wonderful time. It was good for Angelina to see her family being happy again. And it was good for her to have a chance to see some of her very favourite people from the village, people she had known all of her short life. Each one came and sat with her for a time, smiling and talking, and trying to act like nothing was wrong, yet she could see another story in their eyes, especially when they were across the room, talking to Mummy and Daddy, occasionally glancing in her direction. That was okay; she understood that it was scary for them. Still, it was nice to spend some time with them. Some of the children offered to play a game with her, but she was too ill and had to decline.

So the children just sat near Angelina, drinking soda and eating goodies, keeping their little friend company, and for the most part, they remained very quiet.

Over the next few days, it became increasingly difficult for the family to feign cheerfulness around Angelina, who grew more weak and more grey in colour each day.

On Christmas Eve, however, she awoke and seemed a little brighter, which was a thrill for the family, yet they were afraid to hope that this was more than just a temporary reprieve. She laughed more than she had done in a long time, and they all thought she had the faintest bit of rosy colour in her cheeks. Her eyes even sparkled a little throughout the day, and by the evening, she had begun to seem more like her old self.

They all thought it must be a Christmas miracle, and with each passing hour, they found themselves daring to hope a little more.

Even James found himself singing the Christmas carols along with the CD that evening, and he was smiling and talking more than anyone had seen him do in ages.

During the day and into the evening, more friends had dropped in for a cup of hot cider or a glass of wine. The mood in the house was lighter and happier than it had been in a long time, and it felt so good! It looked like their prayers had been answered, and Angelina was, indeed, going to improve, at least for a while. And who knew? With advancing medical research, maybe in time, there would be a cure.

But for the moment, her family and those who knew and loved her just felt relief at the turnaround, and Christmas Eve was a delightful, cheerful and truly wonderful day.

By the time the last visitor left, it was much later than Angelina was used to being awake, but there she sat, curled up on the settee with Frank, her eyes shining as she smiled.

"Oh, Mama! It was such a perfect Christmas Eve, wasn't it?" she exclaimed.

"Yes, Little Angel, it couldn't have been nicer! And we are so happy to see you feeling better!!"

"Yes, I do feel better today. I've been sick such a long time," said the girl, as Kathy picked her up and began to carry her upstairs to bed.

Once Angelina had been tucked in, everyone went to say goodnight as usual, and with Teddy curled up in her arms, and Frank curled up at her feet, the sweet little girl drifted off into a peaceful slumber.

Her parents and her brothers sat up for some time by the roaring fire, having hot drinks while carols played softly in the background. No one had much to say, and each silently gave thanks for this wonderful blessing, until the fire began to die and it was time to go to bed.

The hugs and kisses amongst them that night were extra warm and meaningful; it was amazing what a little hope could do, and it was surprising to the family that Angelina's situation had brought them closer together, and actually had allowed them to feel some sense of happiness again. Everyone went to bed feeling renewed and rejuvenated, eager for a perfect Christmas Day to arrive.

It was Elijah who woke the family before the sun rose. Realizing what day it was, he leapt out of bed and ran through the hallway yelling, "Happy Christmas, everyone! Time to get up! It's Christmas morning!" Having gone to bed rather late, there were three very sleepy heads poking out of bedroom doors when Elijah would not stop calling to his family to get up. The only one who did not make an appearance was Angelina, so Elijah opened her door and said, "Wake up, Sleepyhead! Come and see what Father Christmas left for you!"

A head full of dark curls popped up from the pillow, and the little girl rubbed her eyes and yawned. In his excitement, Elijah did not wait for her to get up, and instead, went bounding down the stairs to the sitting room. It took several minutes for everyone to gather there; Robert was busy making a pot of coffee and getting juice for everyone, Kathy built another fire and got a plate of muffins together, which she placed on a table in the sitting room so that everyone could have a little snack while they took their time opening presents.

Angelina was the last to arrive. She came padding down the stairs, Teddy tucked under her arm as he was every morning. Still half-asleep, she climbed onto her father's lap, while Mummy was still puttering with juice and muffins. Finally, Elijah asked excitedly, "Is everyone ready?"

And the unanimous answer was "Yes!"

With that, James and Elijah, seated on the floor by the tree, began to pass the gifts around, one at a time, taking turns with family members, so that everyone could watch as each gift was opened and admired. There were many oohs and aaahs, hugs and kisses, and lots of 'thank yous' that morning before they were finally finished. Angelina was especially excited to see that Father Christmas had granted both of her wishes. Her family had, indeed, been much happier since she had seen him, and he had also left a beautiful Raggedy Ann doll which was almost as big as she was. She could not have been more happy than she was on that morning.

As the boys cleaned up the mess of wrapping paper and empty boxes, Robert went to make breakfast and a fresh pot of coffee, while Kathy went and scooped up little Angelina into her arms and held her on her lap.

"You look rather sleepy, my Angel. Are you tired?" asked the concerned mother.

"Yes, Mama, I am. I stayed up so late! And then Elijah woke us up so early!"

"Well, Daddy's going to be a while making breakfast, so why don't you just cuddle up here and have a nap?" And with that, Kathy pulled at a quilt that lay across the back of the settee. Covering Angelina and herself with it, she held the girl close.

As Angelina drifted off to sleep, she said, "The angel made my wish come true, Mama. I got to see another Christmas."

And with a lump in her throat, and tears welling up in her eyes, Kathy gave quiet thanks for this blessing.

The boys had wandered off to their rooms with their new treasures, and since Angelina had fallen asleep, Robert postponed making breakfast. Bringing a large, steaming cupful of fresh coffee to his wife, he set it down on the table next to her, and after stoking the fire, sank into a wing-backed chair beside the settee. Sitting quietly while sipping his coffee and holding Kathy's hand, he gazed at his sleeping daughter, safely curled up on her mother's lap and tucked under the quilt.

The two parents barely spoke. They were content to sit together on this beautiful Christmas morning, watching Angelina sleep, silently counting their many blessings. One or the other of them made the occasional comment about the day, the dinner preparations, or about the gifts that had been given and received.

Kathy was in the middle of telling Robert how much she loved one of the gifts he had given her, when suddenly, she stopped partway through a sentence, a puzzled expression on her face before it changed to one of fear. She cast her glance downward at her daughter and said sharply, "Angelina? Angelina!"

As his wife began to shake the child, trying to rouse her, Robert leapt to his feet, adrenalin pumping through his body. Panic-stricken, he kept shouting at Kathy to tell him what was wrong.

But Kathy would not reply. She was frantic, her voice becoming high-pitched as she strained to control her terror. "Something's wrong! Robert! What's wrong?"

Robert leaned down and gently took the child from her mother and laid her across his own lap. He shook her gently, calling her name, and then Kathy saw him do the unthinkable. He felt for a pulse.

Searching his face, desperate to wake from this nightmare, she pleaded with him to tell her that Angelina was all right. But all Robert could do was pull the very still little girl to his chest and cry.

Four

It had been difficult to arrange a funeral to take place before New Year's Eve. Because of the holidays, friends and extended family who lived far away had trouble getting flights, and it was both a blessing and a curse that the Lanes had to wait six days to bury their beloved Little Angel. The blessing was, of course, that they could not bear to see her put into the ground, and they could allow themselves some measure of denial about her death. The curse was that they wanted the horrific event to be over, and the waiting seemed unbearable.

Over the days between Christmas and New Year's Eve, the family was inundated with phone calls and people dropping by, offering their condolences and their help. The refrigerator and freezer were overflowing with food, and Kathy found it odd that she should be wondering how she would ever know which dish belonged to whom when it came time to return them.

No one saw much of James during those days. It was awfully quiet in his room, too. His parents and his brother tried at various times to speak with him, but most of the time, they were told to go away if he answered at all.

Although Elijah missed his sister more than he felt he could bear, he seemed to be coping with it better than everyone else because of his spiritual beliefs. He truly believed that there was a reason, or maybe several, why Angelina had to die, and he knew that it was not for them to understand. It was only for them to accept. This did not mean that he wasn't still just a young boy, grieving over losing his little sister, but his beliefs significantly helped him to get through the darkest days. He wished desperately that he could make his family understand and share his beliefs, because he was certain that if they did, it would give them some measure of peace.

Elijah found himself trying to comfort his family, although nothing he did seemed to make much of a difference. His attempt to share his belief that Angelina's death happened for a reason was met with a sharp retort from Kathy, and total silence from Robert. And James...well, James did not even allow him to introduce the subject. Elijah soon realized that all he could do was offer his parents some comfort with his physical presence, with hugs, and with trying to make things a little easier for them.

He made coffee and took it to them. He sat in silence with them. He put light meals together, but no one seemed to eat very much, if anything. He wanted so badly to talk about Angelina; he thought that if they stopped talking about her, then not only would she be dead, she would be forgotten. But no one in the family understood, and it seemed her name was suddenly off limits.

This was terribly painful for Elijah; he was certain that it would also upset Angelina to see her family like this, locking themselves away from each other, and refusing to allow any mention of her name. But what was he to do? It seemed there was no answer.

The only one who really seemed to appreciate his presence was Frank. She missed her 'Mummy', having been with Angelina almost continuously since her arrival in the family a few months earlier. Elijah stepped in as 'Daddy' and made sure that she was fed and had lots of cuddles. It made him feel closer to his sister, too, as he had long conversations with Frank about Angelina, and in fact, with Angelina herself. He had taken to holing up in her room, sitting on Angelina's bed with the kitten, and he chatted away endlessly about his memories of his sweet little sister, and about his feelings and what was happening for him and the family since she died. It made him feel so much better to speak to her, and many times, he was certain that he could feel Angelina in the room with the two of them.

Kathy had been so hysterical and distraught that Robert had written a prescription for tranquilizers for his wife, sending a neighbour to the pharmacy to collect them. She was absolutely inconsolable, and resisted all attempts by him or anyone else to offer her some comfort. Hiding in their bedroom almost all the time, she only made a rare appearance as family members began to arrive from out of town. After a brief time, however, she would always retreat back to the privacy of her room, where she could grieve and cry alone.

Robert did his best to field phone calls and visitors, and he was left to plan most of the funeral by himself. He was unable to elicit even a small amount of input from Kathy; she was so overwhelmed with grief, it just was not in her to do it. In the end, it was Elijah who offered some helpful ideas. Robert struggled to take care of everything, but he felt as though he were in a rapidly sinking ship.

After having great difficulty in getting a flight, Robert's sister, Sandra, finally arrived and took over, lightening Robert's load considerably. Sandra was a very sensitive woman who had no children of her own, but loved her niece and nephews dearly. She had lost her own husband years earlier, and well understood grief, and how it felt to lose someone so close. Having been down that road, she was able to draw on her experience and help her brother's family in many different ways during this horribly dark time.

It was a huge relief to Robert to have his sister there, answering the phone, helping with decisions, with meals and seeing to the running of the house. People were wandering in and out almost continuously, all well-meaning, of course, but sometimes, he wished that they would just go away and leave them in peace. But he was well aware that even if they left, there would be no peace, not with their sweet Angelina lying in a funeral home, awaiting burial.

The old feelings of guilt had returned with a vengeance when Angelina died. He had been so thrilled upon her arrival in this world, feeling as though he had been absolved of his responsibility for Kathy's accident and her inability to bear children, but of course, it had not gone quite as they had planned when she was born an unhealthy child with a very uncertain future. He had always clung to the hope that there would be some treatment or cure which would allow them a happy outcome, but apparently, it was not meant to be.

Being the one upon whom his family was relying to stay strong at this time had helped to keep his feelings at bay; he was able to swallow them and do the things that needed to be done. But with the arrival of his sister, who relieved him of many of his responsibilities, he was able to chew on his guilt once again. It tore him apart to see Kathy hiding in their room, living on tranquilizers, not even allowing him to hold her while she wept. It was hard for him to believe that they used to turn to each other for support and comfort in their struggles; suddenly, they seemed to be miles apart, unable to share anything at all.

And James; oh, how he worried about the deeply sensitive and introverted young man. He feared that the boy's anger was going to destroy him. One morning, just after Angelina died, Robert found him asleep on her bed, clutching her Teddy, Frank at his feet. Knowing that his son would be terribly embarrassed to have been caught like that, he closed the door quietly, then turned and wept bitter tears for the lad's breaking heart.

Robert recognized that Elijah was not getting much attention from his family, but he seemed to be coping fairly well, all things considered. Robert did not have the energy to seek out the boy and be sure that he was really doing as well as he appeared to be. Robert realized that he may be in some denial about Elijah's emotional state, but he was simply unable to reach out to the boy at that time. And this only compounded his guilt.

Sandra saw what a mess this family was in; she saw the fractures clearly enough. It was as though Angelina's death amplified every issue that each of them had, and she feared that if someone didn't do something -- and soon -- the family would fall apart.

She knew it was not that they didn't love each other; in that regard, they were fine. But there had been too much left unsaid for far too long, and the damage was only getting worse.

New Year's Eve arrived, and with it came a snowy, windy, very bleak morning; the weather certainly suited the mood of the Lane family. Sandra made a simple breakfast, but they struggled to put a small amount of it into their stomachs before getting dressed.

Kathy stumbled through the morning, wishing she could take more tranquilizers because the normal dose just wasn't numbing the pain. No longer could she try to pretend that Angelina was going to come bouncing down the stairs and run into her arms; she knew that this was the day she was burying her sweet little girl. The reality was overwhelming, and she felt as though no amount of medication was going to be able to get her through it.

Robert, stoic as he could possibly be, choked back screams as he continued to hide his pain and be strong for his family. He was desperate for the opportunity to fall apart, to break down and cry, but he knew that it was impossible. He longed to hold his wife, seeking comfort in her arms, but every time he went to touch her, she recoiled, afraid that his embrace would allow her to completely shatter. Unaware of her reasons for pushing him away, all he could glean from such behaviour was that she held him responsible in some way for Angelina's death. Perhaps she saw him as he saw himself -- the deficient and incompetent doctor, unable to save his own child's life.

Elijah was dreading the service, never having been to a funeral in his ten years, and although he believed that this was all meant to happen, it did nothing to help him face seeing his sister closed up in a wooden box and put into the cold and frozen ground. He had not wanted to see her the previous night when the family went to say their goodbyes, but by the time they got back home, he realized that it had been a mistake and he knew he had to do it before the funeral. He had to tell Angelina a proper goodbye. He did not know what to expect, never having seen a dead person before, and as spiritual a child as he was, he was still just a boy, and the notion of seeing his little sister in a coffin was terrifying.

As intuitive as he was, he knew that his parents were incapable of helping him with his fears and worries, and he never felt more alone in his life. Elijah had always loved his Aunt Sandra very much, and in some ways, she was like a second mother to her brother's children. Yet at this particular time, he was afraid that if his parents saw him treating her in that role, it might upset them.

James was so angry and silent, he was beyond knowing what to do with himself. He was enraged that the Dream Child had turned out to be such a nightmare for his family, and after all they had gone through before she arrived, it was especially infuriating that she died. He was furious with Angelina for dying, and guilt-ridden for being so angry with her for putting them through this hell. And he was livid because she had taken away the biggest source of light and joy in his life, as well as his only sense of spirituality.

And if there was a God, James was saving the worst of his rage for a Supreme Being who could kill a sweet and innocent child. The last thing James wanted that day was to go to the funeral; he wanted to run as far away as he could possibly get from the service, his family, Angelina's dead body in a coffin and the big hole in the cold ground that was waiting to receive it.

The limousine arrived to collect Kathy, Robert, the boys, and Sandra. Suddenly, the funeral seemed a little more real, and the horror of facing it was amplified with the blast of icy wind and snow that hit them as they left the house.

Settling into their seats, each lost in his or her own thoughts, they sat in silence as the long, black car slowly made its way to the funeral home.

Once there, they were given the opportunity for a few final moments with Angelina before other mourners arrived to pay their final respects. Elijah was nervous and uncomfortable, but there was no one he could tell. He watched from a distance as his parents stood beside the coffin, his mother weeping silently into a handkerchief, his father's face reflecting heart-breaking pain while he stood, unmoving as he gazed down at his little girl.

James refused to see Angelina again; the previous night had been hard enough on him. The image of her face, as she lay on the pink satin in her coffin, was burned into his memory. He would never forget her dark curls, or how they framed her delicate face, a little pink bow tied into them on the right side of her head. Her slightly pink cheeks and lips, giving her the illusion of a sleeping, healthy child, only served to enrage him further. She had been pale and looked so ill when she died; why did they have to pretend that she was perfectly well, which only made her death seem even more senseless, if that was possible?

No, James had no need to see that perfect little face again. He wandered off by himself for a while, leaving his family with Angelina.

When his parents had finished saying goodbye to his sister, Elijah rose from his chair, but then hesitated. Uncertain and afraid, he suddenly found himself wishing he were anywhere but there. He did not want to look at his sister in that coffin, yet he knew from his reaction last night that if he did not do it now, he would never get another chance, and he was certain he would regret it for the rest of his life.

Elijah felt his feet moving under him, but it was as if they had a will of their own. They seemed to be transporting him closer and closer to Angelina in her casket, though in his head, he was screaming at them to stop. But they did not. And before long, there he was, looking down at his sweet little sister as she lay peacefully in death. He felt a mixture of emotions, among them relief that she looked happy and healthy again. He could have sworn she was just sleeping, and he felt compelled to give her a kiss, but he was afraid. There was a sense that she was going to sit up and ask him to play with her, followed by a wave of tremendous sadness, as he understood that she would never say that, or anything else, again.

It was this realization which prompted the boy to feel compelled to lean down and give his sister one last, sweet kiss on her lips. They were cool under his own, and for this, he had been unprepared. As he stood, still leaning down over his beloved sister, a few tears escaped his eyes and came to rest on her soft cheek.

He wanted to fall apart and weep openly, but he feared that his parents could not cope with a display of his grief. And so, he remained very alone in it, and swallowing hard on the lump in this throat, and choking back any more tears, he whispered a quiet goodbye to his little sister before turning and walking away.

The family had opted to sit separately from everyone else, behind a screen so that they could see and hear everything, without being seen themselves. It was going to be hard enough to deal with their own feelings, and the family dynamics, without feeling countless sets of sympathetic eyes staring at them, or seeing pitying expressions on all those faces.

It was not so easy, however, at the cemetery. There, the family stood with everyone else in the biting wind, next to the grave, beside which stood Angelina's casket, so tiny and white, with beautiful, brightly coloured flowers covering the top. A little heart on the side bore her photograph. Her parents and James did their best not to look at it, while Elijah could not take his eyes off the beautiful image of his sister, happy and smiling, her spirit shining through.

Angelina's parents and brothers heard almost nothing that was said during either of the two services. All of them were lost in thought, struggling to get through such a gut-wrenching ordeal, desperately wishing that the funeral would end. And finally, mercifully, it did.

The ride back home in the limousine was just as awful as the first trip had been, but the family had gone from anxious, nervous and vibrating to relieved, drained and overwhelmingly sad. The reality could no longer be denied. Angelina would never be with them again.

Arriving back at the cottage, the Lane family knew that it would soon be filled with mourners. Kathy and James would have been quite happy to tell them all to go away, but Robert and Elijah needed to talk about little Angelina. For days, they had been forced to keep their feelings to themselves, but finally, they would have a chance to grieve along with others. If only they had spoken about how they were feeling, they could have been leaning on each other. Yet both had chosen to remain silent, thinking it was the best decision they could make.

As it happened, James did make a brief appearance, just long enough to tolerate a few words of sympathy from some of their guests, and as soon as he could possibly manage it, he disappeared into his bedroom, but not before finding a bottle of whisky to take with him. It was to be his first experience with alcohol, but he had heard that it helps to numb painful feelings, and if ever there was a time for shutting off all feeling, it was on that horrendous day.

Kathy managed to stay with her guests for a while longer than James had done, knowing that relatives and friends would be wanting to offer their condolences. The last thing she needed was to have them seeking her out and invading the privacy of her bedroom; it seemed best if she could put up with their questions and their talk of Angelina for a while. But before she could cope with any of that, as soon as they walked back into the house, she headed for her bathroom and got another tranquilizer. Images of Angelina's little white coffin, sitting beside the open grave, waiting to be lowered into the ground kept rolling through her head. She felt certain that she would never see anything but that picture again.

And what was worse, she was horrified to find that she was struggling to recall Angelina's face and her voice. What kind of mother was she, she asked herself over and over again. How on earth could she forget her beloved little girl's face and voice at all, never mind only days after her death?

Swallowing her tranquilizer, she prepared for the crowds of people who would soon converge upon the grieving family.

Five

As the weeks passed, not much changed for the Lane family. Elijah spent a lot of time in Angelina's bedroom, her unused Christmas presents, still there in a basket where they had been put on the day she died. The big Raggedy Ann lay on her bed with Teddy, and Frank was often found curled up on the large doll, as if she thought it was her 'Mummy'. Elijah felt close to his sister there; her room eased the chill of his loneliness. Speaking to her helped him to miss her just a little less. Unbeknownst to the lad, little Angelina was, indeed, there, trying her hardest to speak with him, but because they were both young, they were inexperienced with this kind of communication.

Kathy insisted that nothing be touched in the girl's room, so Elijah always had to be very careful not to change anything about the way it looked. He tried not to get caught in there, because he was uncertain about what his mother's response might be. She spent most of her time in her own room, and because of the layout of the house, when he heard her stirring, he was able to sneak out of Angelina's room very quickly without her noticing that he had been inside.

On rare occasion, when no one was home, Kathy dared go into Angelina's room. She was always torn between the overwhelming pain of these 'visits', and the unbearable need to be with her daughter. Angelina's presence in the room was unmistakable; sometimes, Kathy risked the pain to feel closer to the child. Picking up Teddy, she would sit on Angelina's bed, and sob wildly as she clutched the bear close to her chest, unaware that her sweet daughter truly was there, stroking her mother's arm or hair, offering comfort that Kathy could not feel.

On these occasions, she would wail and sometimes scream, grateful that they lived in the country, so that even if the windows were open, there was no one to hear her indescribable grief.

James had taken to sneaking bottles of alcohol to his room whenever possible. His parents had always kept a well-stocked bar, and when Angelina died, many people brought even more. There was so much of it in the house that he was certain they would not notice any of it missing. People were right; alcohol did numb the pain somewhat. But it also allowed his anger to bubble and boil just beneath the surface; he could not suppress it as easily as when he was not drinking. He found himself playing angrier music, writing angrier lyrics.

His rage had begun to consume him; it was eating him alive. He seemed to need to feed it; he was unwilling to part with it, and alcohol kept adding fuel to the fire. And because of this, it was impossible for him to know how many times his little sister was right there on his bed, watching him, listening to him, and understanding him. She longed for the day that he would know she was with him, but if it happened at all, it was apparent that it would not be for a very long time.

Once Robert went back to work, he began to spend increasingly long hours at the hospital, avoiding Angelina's room when he was at home. If her door was open as he passed it, he would reach in and gently close it without looking inside. It had become his routine to leave the house in the morning before his family was up, and whenever possible, he arrived late in the evening. He kept himself so busy that he seldom felt Angelina with him, trying to console him.

Many times, he sat in the big, swivel chair in his office, leaning back, facing the ceiling, eyes closed and recalling memories of his little girl. And on those occasions, Angelina seized the opportunity to try to speak with her daddy, climbing onto his lap, and hoping he would know she was there. Sometimes, he thought he felt her with him, but he was very skeptical about life after death, and chose, instead, to believe that it was merely wishful thinking.

On weekends, Robert found excuses to be out of the house, unable to cope with James's angry silence and Kathy's desire to be left entirely alone. Sometimes, Elijah asked his father if they could do something together, and usually, Robert complied. But the invitations never came from the father.

Too consumed by guilt and feelings of inadequacy was he to notice that Elijah still needed him, until the lad piped up, asking for some of his father's attention.

When they went off together, it almost felt like the old days, before Angelina died. Being with Elijah was good for Robert; he found himself relaxing a little, and sometimes even smiled or laughed a bit. But he was too quiet, and still seemed rather tense. Angelina was so happy when her daddy went out with her brother; they both really needed to be together, and it was good to see them a wee bit happy again.

Angelina knew that Elijah was going to be all right, but in the meantime, it made her sad to see that he was the only one who really understood why she had to leave. Knowing that he could help his family through this terrible time, it was upsetting for her to see each of them lost and feeling completely alone, when Elijah could ease their pain. Not only were the fractures not healing, they were growing bigger and making the family more fragile than it had ever been before.

The Little Angel had been busy adjusting to Life on The Other Side, since arriving there on Christmas morning. It did not alarm or upset her to be there; she was in a beautiful, peaceful place, where she had been met by her two Grannies, a Grandpa, and other relatives and family friends. They were all standing in a circle, waiting with outstretched arms as she drifted through the warm, bright light and it was a delightful reunion. There was no fear, no worry, only a rapidly growing understanding and acceptance of the fact that this was meant to be.

During her first few days on The Other Side, Angelina was getting acquainted with her new surroundings, but she did check in on her family from time to time and could see how devastated they were about losing her. Of course, it made her very sad for them, but she knew that in time, they would realize that it had to happen. Even though they might not have understood until they joined her, they would still come to that point eventually.

She was there, at the funeral home, when they said goodbye to her, and during the service, and it warmed her heart to see the love that each of them felt for her. Though it saddened her to see their pain, she knew that it was necessary, a part of the whole process. Angelina was right there with them during those times, and at the cemetery, trying to let them know that she was with them. But they were too lost in their grief to notice.

The Little Angel had gone to her Teachers, wanting to know how she could help her family. But the only answer she was given was that she had much to learn about how everything worked between the two realms. They said she had to be patient, and that in time, all would be revealed. In the meantime, they urged her to watch her family, and to try to communicate with them, for this was a very difficult skill to master. What made it harder was that her family had to be open to receiving her messages. And from what Angelina could see so far, none of them was capable of it, except Elijah. She was certain that once he had some time to heal from her death, and after she had practiced for a while, she would, indeed, be able to communicate with him. Excited about the prospect, Angelina was only too happy to work on learning this new skill.

It was well into January before Elijah decided he could go back to school. In some ways, it would be a relief. The cottage had become such an oppressive, dark and sad place to be, except for the times he spent talking to Angelina (and hoping she was listening) in her bedroom. He was certain that he was going to have some difficulty concentrating on his studies, and he wasn't sure about how he would be treated by the other children and his teachers, but he realized that it was time to try to get on with his life. He felt able to do this, knowing that it did not mean he didn't love or miss his little sister, and especially because he was certain that she knew that.

Still, he was a bit anxious on his first day back. He awoke before his alarm went off, and lay in bed, contemplating what the morning would bring. He did not feel as though he would be able to eat much breakfast, and decided that he would pack a good-sized lunch, in hopes that he would have faced the worst of his fears and got through those first uncomfortable sympathetic stares and words by that time.

Kathy managed to be up and in the kitchen with Elijah that morning, but her forced smile and her tight expression were unmistakable. He appreciated her efforts to get back to being

‘Mummy’, and understood that it was going to be a long time before she was anything like she used to be.

Kathy was working her way through the kitchen, making breakfast for Elijah while he put together a lunch for himself, and she was unaware that he was watching her. While she was in the midst of laying the table, he stopped what he was doing, turning to her as she passed him. Without a word, he put his arms out, and held her around her waist, giving his mother a warm and loving hug. It felt so good, a pure expression of his love for her, coming straight from his heart, but it was cut short.

Kathy’s mind had been on Angelina as she was laying the table for breakfast. She was painfully aware of the empty space where her little girl’s plate and glass should be. At every meal, this was like a knife in the grieving mother’s heart, and on this occasion, it was just at that moment that Elijah had reached out for his mother and hugged her.

Completely caught off guard, Kathy did not know what to do. For a split second, she thought it was Angelina there, hugging her again, since her thoughts had been with the girl as she was desperately missing her. And instantly following was the realization that it was not her beloved Little Angel, but rather, it was Elijah. It felt as though she had been slammed with a dose of reality, reinforcing the fact that Angelina was dead.

As quickly as she could, Kathy pulled herself away from Elijah's embrace, mumbling something about having to hurry and get ready. Had it been audible, she would have heard his little heart break, yet again.

Elijah's face fell, and his arms hung at his sides. He stared after his mother as she turned her back to him. He did not see that she was struggling to suppress a million tears, nor did she recognize this in him. With a heavy sigh, the boy turned his attention once again to his lunch, less certain now that he would be able to eat it.

Within a few minutes, Kathy had got breakfast on the table, and poured a glass of juice for her son. As usual, she barely ate anything herself, and mostly just pushed the food around her plate while attempting to make small talk with Elijah. Noticing that he was extremely quiet and seemed reluctant to speak, it felt like there was an elephant in the room, which neither of them was willing to discuss, and both were trying to ignore.

Finally, Kathy spoke. "I'm sorry, Elijah. I didn't mean to push you away. You caught me at a particularly weak moment, and..." Her voice trailed off, as she found herself unable to say what she was thinking, certain that it would create floods of tears which she did not think she could handle.

"It's okay, Mum," was the boy's reply, although really, he didn't mean it. It really wasn't okay, but he knew that his mother was incapable of hearing about his feelings just then, and who knew how long it might be before that changed? There was no point in telling her how lonely he was, how much he missed her, how much he needed her. It would just make her feel worse, knowing that she was neglecting him to the point of causing him pain.

Kathy's relief was visible when Elijah let her off the hook. Sometimes, she was able to see what was happening to him as she was being swallowed by her grief, yet she felt unable to change or control anything about herself in a way that might help her boy. Mostly, she simply relied on the fact that he was a very wise and spiritual child, certain that he understood her, and could be patient, waiting for her to get better.

A few minutes passed and the two were silent, Elijah eating very little, and Kathy eating even less, until finally, the boy stood up and said, "I'd better get going. The school bus will be here shortly."

He reached for their dishes and began to clear the table, when Kathy put out her hand. Touching his forearm, she stopped him. "It's okay, I'll do it. Thank you, Eli." And giving him a sad smile, she had a moment of really remembering her love for this sweet boy.

Elijah put the breakfast dishes by the sink, choking back tears which struggled to erupt after his mother's unexpected display of affection. He was happy to leave the kitchen as quickly as possible, hurrying to the bathroom to brush his teeth, then collecting his lunch and his backpack before putting on his coat and boots. He wanted to give his mother a kiss goodbye, and tell her to have a good day like he used to do, but after the hug, he could guess that the kiss would not be well received, and he was certain that a wish for a good day, albeit very sincere, would be seen as a slap in the face.

Instead, he gave her a little smile, told her he would see her after school, and headed out into the chilly winter morning.

Kathy watched through the kitchen window as Elijah made his way down the snowy drive, his head hanging, looking as though he carried the weight of the world on his shoulders. She felt pangs of guilt as she saw him standing by the mailbox, waiting for the school bus, knowing that he felt very much alone. But between her guilt and his loneliness, it was more than she could bear, and refilling her cup with coffee, she headed back to bed, but not before taking another tranquilizer.

Elijah heard the school bus before he saw it; he had been staring at the ground, lost in thought, remembering the days when he and James would be waving and making faces at Angelina, as she peered out the window at them while they waited for the bus. Sometimes, when the weather was warm, if Angelina felt well enough, she would skip out to the end of the drive with her brothers, and play with them until they climbed onto the bus and headed for school.

Until he was standing there by the mailbox on that frosty morning, it had not occurred to Elijah that this would be his first morning waiting for the bus without Angelina beside him or waving from the house. And without James as well, their little sister's absence was hauntingly exaggerated.

"Oh, Angelina!" whispered Elijah, fighting tears as the bus rumbled along, coming closer. "I miss you so much!"

The loving energy behind her brother's bittersweet words carried them quickly through the Heavens, until they reached the Little Angel's ears. Immediately, she went to investigate, knowing that one of these times, her reply would actually be heard.

But it was not to be on this occasion. Angelina saw Elijah climbing the big steps of the school bus, his head hanging, and she was certain that she saw him wipe a tear from his eye.

The Lane family was one of the first on the bus route, so there were not too many children seated when Elijah got on and sat down. Most of them were people from around the village, people he had already seen during the time since Angelina died, so he was relieved. These first big steps, waiting alone for the bus, and facing going back to school, were hard enough; he was glad to find at least one easier part.

But as the bus rolled along the route, collecting children who lived quite far from the Lanes, and who did not socialize with them, Elijah finally got the answers to his questions about how he would be treated.

With each face Elijah saw, he was anxious, wondering what reaction he was going to get. Thankfully, no one gave him any trouble, or asked too many questions. Mostly, it was just quiet on the bus. In fact, too quiet. Some of the children looked at him with pity, others gave shy smiles, and still others seemed not to notice or care that he was there; to them, it was just like any other day.

There were many whispers, and a fair amount of pointing as Elijah left the bus and made his way to the classroom. Some kids said 'Hi', others who were talking in groups suddenly stopped speaking mid-sentence as they saw him approaching, and stared as he passed, their necks straining as their heads followed his movements. He heard snippets of conversations, words like ‘dead’ and ‘sister’ seemed to leap out at him, as though his ears were now trained only to hear words on the subject of Angelina.

Elijah knew that he was an oddity; not many children his age, and certainly not children in his school, had lost a little sister. He understood that there were many reasons that this was likely to be a really big deal for the other students, among them the fear that they, too, might die while still young. But he was not prepared for some of what happened.

Jimmy Watson was one of those kids who did not have many friends, and it was easy to figure out why that was so. It seemed that Jimmy spent his days trying to discover the best ways in which he could be annoying. He was always teasing people, and he was unbearably rude. He would say or do just about anything if he thought it was going to get a reaction out of someone. Most people said they hated Jimmy, but that word was not in Elijah’s vocabulary, not even for Jimmy, no matter how nasty he could be.

It felt very strange to be back; he felt like the new kid on a first day, although he had gone to school with these children his whole life. Elijah was just walking into the classroom, having left his coat and boots in the cloakroom inside the door, when he heard Jimmy's voice, bellowing at him from across the room.

"Hey, Elijah! How come your stupid little sister died?"

All conversation in the room stopped immediately. Heads spun to look at either Jimmy, or Elijah, or back and forth between the two. Everyone wondered how Elijah would respond. Some jumped in and told Jimmy to shutup and not be so awful. Elijah said nothing, attempting to look as though he had not heard it, but of course, everyone knew he had.

He continued walking toward his desk. Jimmy had the floor now; he knew he had everyone's attention, and they all knew how he lived for that.

"Hey! I asked you a question!" he called. "Not gonna answer me? Why not? Did you kill that little brat? Boy, I wish my little sister was dead. Tell me how you did it. Wanna help me kill mine, too?"

Elijah stopped in his tracks, his face showing shock and pain like no one present could describe. Everyone was too stunned to do anything for a few moments; then the classroom erupted as many of the children went after Jimmy, who was laughing wildly, pointing at Elijah, taunting him with more talk of how delightful it would be to have a dead sister.

A couple of larger boys went after Jimmy, one of them saying he was going to tear his stupid head off. Just then, the teacher came in, only to find her class in chaos, a group of children crowding around Elijah, trying to help him as best a bunch of 10-year-olds could in such a circumstance, and a fist fight occurring with Jimmy Watson at the center of it.

"What's going on here?!" shouted Mrs. Robinson, a look of utter disbelief on her face.

Several children tried to speak at once, anxious to tell their teacher just how horrible Jimmy Watson had been to Elijah. When she finally heard the story, Mrs. Robinson's mouth fell open. She was obviously furious with Jimmy, and her face bore an expression that the children had never seen before. Nor did they ever want to see it again. She could not send Jimmy to the office fast enough, and having done so, she turned her attention very quickly to Elijah.

Everyone was silent. Mrs. Robinson's voice softened as she spoke to him, asking him to step outside with her. Eyes brimming with tears, and wishing the children would not notice, Elijah walked from his place at the back of the class, then crossed the room to the door as he followed his teacher. He'd had more than enough of being stared at for one day; in fact, for a lifetime.

Once out in the empty corridor, Mrs. Robinson took Elijah by the shoulders. Upon seeing the tears that were welling up in his eyes, she asked him if it was all right to give him a hug. The lump in his throat prevented him answering, except to give her a nod of approval, and as she embraced the boy, he could no longer contain the floods of tears that had remained buried for too long.

Although Elijah was silent while he sobbed in his teacher's arms, inside himself he was crying out to Angelina. And it was not long before she was aware that her brother needed her. She found him, crying as he squeezed Mrs. Robinson tightly, as if he was afraid one of them would blow away if he let go.

The Little Angel stood beside her distraught brother, doing her best to communicate with him. She put her little arms around him the best she could, with his teacher hugging him already, and remembering what she had learned, put all her energy into making him hear what she had to say: "I'm here, Elijah. I'm right here." Over and over again, she sent this message to him, and prayed that maybe this time, she could make him hear.

The weeping boy suddenly pulled away from his teacher, looking very embarrassed and apologizing as he wiped his face with the backs of his hands. Mrs. Robinson reached into her pocket and pulling out a couple of folded tissues, handed them to Elijah. And as he dried his tears and blew his nose, he felt as though he and his teacher were being watched. Looking up and down the corridor, he saw no one else there, but the feeling never left him. He comforted himself with the belief that maybe, just maybe, Angelina was there with him.

"Thank you, Mrs. Robinson. I'm all right now," Elijah smiled.

"Are you sure, Elijah? Is there anything I can do for you?" Mrs. Robinson was most concerned about him.

"Yes, I'll be okay. I just need a few minutes and I'll be inside."

"All right, then. If you need anything at all, you just let me know. I can only imagine what you're going through right now and you will have lots of support here to help you. Never mind people like Jimmy; you know how he likes to push buttons. And if you have any more trouble, with him or anyone else, you tell me or the Head Master immediately, all right?"

"I promise," replied Elijah. "Thank you. And please, Mrs. Robinson, would you make sure that my parents don't hear about this?"

Mrs. Robinson tilted her head, a puzzled expression on her face as she leaned a little closer to the boy. "Why don't you want them to know, Elijah?" she asked, obviously deeply concerned.

Elijah was silent for a moment. He did not want to violate his parents' privacy by telling his teacher about what was going on at home, yet he was well aware that it would cause a lot of unnecessary stress for them if they knew what had happened at school that day. The ten-year-old struggled, not knowing just how much he should divulge, but wanting to protect his family.

"My parents are having a really hard time right now," the boy offered. "There's nothing they can do or say to change what Jimmy did this morning, so there's no point in upsetting them. I'll be all right, Mrs. Robinson. I understand about people like Jimmy," Elijah explained, although he really didn't believe that last part.

Mrs. Robinson paused for a moment, looking intently into the little boy's deep blue eyes. Taking a deep breath and sighing, she replied, "All right, Elijah. If you're sure..."

"Yes, ma'am, I am," said Elijah, trying his best to convince her that he meant it.

"Well, if you think that's best. I'll speak to the Head Master right away and be sure that he doesn't ring your family."

"Thank you," replied the boy.

"Is there anything else you want to tell me? Anything else you need?" asked Mrs. Robinson.

"No, ma'am. I'm fine," said Elijah, taking a deep breath and standing as straight and tall as he could.

Giving Elijah a warm smile, the kind teacher turned and headed toward the office without another word.

And with that, the little boy went to wash his face, and a few minutes later, joined his class, taking the first step toward reclaiming his life. And unbeknownst to him, his sweet sister was right by his side for much of that day.

Six

James was rarely out of bed before the early afternoon. He had taken to staying up until the wee hours, playing his guitar and drinking. His friends had begun calling to see if he was interested in going out, but he had wanted only to hide away in his room, and fan the flames of his rage.

He had written many songs during this period, all of them angry and filled with more pain than he thought any human being should have to bear. He thought that by expressing his feelings in this manner, there would be some relief from them, but it seemed that his rage was spewing forth from a bottomless pit.

Robert had spoken with James a time or two regarding getting back to school and trying to get back to a normal life, but the young man's angry eyes and sharp retorts told him that he should leave the subject alone. It seemed that the distance between them grew wider each day, and he had no idea how to reach his son.

As far as James was concerned, he just wanted his father to go away and leave him alone. The last thing he wanted was to get back to school, and life was never going to be normal again, so why would anybody even consider trying to make that happen?

One evening, not long after Elijah had returned to school, there was a knock at the door. Robert went to answer it, and there stood two of James's friends, Mike and Billy. He had not seen them in some time; Robert was always turning them away under James's instruction, and they had given up trying to see their friend for a while.

But now they were back, and Robert welcomed them. This time, he sent them up to James's room, rather than going himself, in hopes that their appearance at his son's door might prompt the boy to get out of the house for a while.

And wasn't he stunned when about ten minutes later, Mike and Billy were coming down the stairs, with James right behind them.

"Hey, Dad, we're goin' out for a while," was all he said as he grabbed his coat and slammed the door behind him.

Robert didn't know what to make of this, but at least, James was out of his room, and was with his friends again. Maybe things were finally going to start to get better.

Mike and Billy were about as surprised as Robert when not only did they get to see their friend again, but persuaded him to join them for an evening out. Billy was 17 and had an old car, which, when he wasn't driving it, usually found him with his head under its hood. He was a bit on the wild side but had a boyish grin that won the hearts of Mums everywhere. They trusted him, and were unaware that he may be more dangerous than they realized. He could be quite charming, and that, in itself, managed to get him off the hook on countless occasions.

Mike was more like James, quiet, serious, very much into making music. He was more easygoing than James, however; they did not share the same temper. Mike had not seen James since Angelina's funeral, and therefore, he had not been aware of how much more angry and volatile his friend had become in the past several weeks.

The first thing Mike and Billy noticed when they saw James was that he did not look well. He had lost weight; his previously slim frame was gaunt, his face pale and drawn. Aside from his appearance, something in him was changed; they were uncertain about exactly what, but they knew this was not the same James they last saw in December. But they were about to find out what was different about their friend.

The three boys went out to Billy's car, opened the doors and got in. Billy put the key in the ignition, started the car and headed down the drive. As he turned onto the road, James, alone in the back seat, pulled out a bottle of whisky that had been hidden in the inside pocket of his winter jacket.

Mike and Billy were shocked when suddenly, a bottle appeared between their heads, handed to them by James in the back. Billy, as wild as he was, was not brave enough to drink while he was driving, especially with the slippery road conditions. Mike, who was 15, same as James, had not yet got into alcohol consumption, and hesitated.

"Aw, c'mon, Mike! It's no big deal! Try a little!" urged James.

"I don't know, mate," hedged Mike. "I got enough trouble these days; I don't need any more."

"What's up?" asked James. "This makes everything better."

"Got trouble at home," said Mike. "My dad split and my parents are getting a divorce."

"What?? Oh, man! Your dad split? I can't believe it!" was James's incredulous reply. "Here, you need this at least as much as I do."

He shoved the bottle toward Mike, who looked at it with great skepticism, as if he could see the potential for this to be a very bad move. Again, James pushed the bottle toward him, saying, "Oh, come on! Just try a little! You'll see, it helps."

"Ya, Mike, what's up with you? Turning into a girl?" teased Billy.

Having had enough of these two, Mike snatched the bottle from James's hand, removed the lid and took a swallow. Shuddering, and blinking hard, he was surprised by the strength of the straight whisky. The others laughed at him, while he shook his head and passed the bottle back to James.

Billy kept driving, asking if his friends had a preference about where they should go or what they should do. James thought they should try to find a party, and Billy, wild streak blazing, hollered, “Woo-hoo! I know just where to go!”

Before long, the three pulled up behind a very seedy looking pub in a small village. It was the kind of place that he was certain would never be frequented by anyone his parents knew, so he was pretty sure he wouldn’t get caught. Although in thinking of it, he decided he didn’t much care about that anyway.

The three climbed out of the car, into the cold winter night. Pulling their coats around them, Mike and James followed Billy as the three hurried to a back door. Billy knocked, and soon, a short, unshaven man appeared, a cigarette dangling from his lips, his huge beer belly covered by a dirty apron. Though he was not a tall man, he was stocky in his build, and appeared to be very powerful. His scowl quickly changed to a wide-eyed smile as he recognized Billy.

Opening the door and standing aside, he cried in a thick Irish accent, “Ah,

Billy! How are ya, lad? Haven't seen ya in a little while!" And he slammed the boy on the back a time or two, as men usually do when they meet.

"Hey, Mad Dog. Yeah, had the car apart again. Always something with that old pig, ya know, so I was stuck till I got it fixed. This here's Mike, and this is my friend, James."

"Mike! James! Good to meet ya, lads! Remember the first rule of coming to this joint, won'tcha? Shut up about it!" He gave the two a rather stern look which didn't last before he broke into another big smile, and with his booming voice, invited them inside.

The boys were happy to get out of the cold. Mad Dog led them to a little room in the back of the pub. There was a pool table in it, and only a couple of dirty tables, along with a few chairs with wobbly, uneven legs. Taking off their coats and hanging them on pegs near the door, the boys sat at one of the tables, while Mad Dog asked, "What's your pleasure?"

Billy said, "The usual for me, Mad Dog, a beer!" And turning to Mike and James, asked, "What do you two want?"

Mike thought for a moment and said, "A beer, same as you, Billy."

"Whisky over here," said James. "Straight up. And make it a double."

Mad Dog's eyes widened. The boy seemed a bit young and inexperienced for such an order. "A double? Straight up?? You sure about that?"

James's anger, always so close to the surface, rather surprised the man as it flashed in the boy's eyes. "Yes! I'm *quite* sure." His tone was most intimidating, even for the big man on the receiving end of it. In an effort to appease the boy's temper, he smiled and said, "Only my finest Irish for you, young James!"

Having poured a good-sized shot of whisky, next he opened two bottles of beer, placed the drinks on a tray and delivered them to the boys. After years of working in a bar, Mad Dog knew people. And he had surely seen his share of angry ones. He seldom saw in anyone the kind of rage he had just seen in this boy. He could not decide whether he should feel sorry for him or intimidated by him. Saying nothing, he placed the drinks in front of the lads, and left them for a while.

James started to relax and loosen up just a little as the evening passed. Mad Dog kept the drinks coming, and in time, James even found himself laughing. But it wasn't the right kind of laughter, or so noticed Mad Dog. It seemed forced and angry somehow; the man wondered just what was this boy's story.

But long ago, he had learned to keep his mouth shut in this business. So he just kept pouring.

After the three had been there a while, Billy excused himself, saying he and Mad Dog had a little business to do. James and Mike saw the two, heads bent together behind the bar, speaking in whispers. It looked like there was some sort of exchange of packages between them, and then Billy rejoined his friends, sat down, and did not offer any explanation. Rather, he changed the subject, leaving Mike and James a bit suspicious.

The hours passed and it was about midnight. Mike looked at his watch and jumped, not realizing the time. "Oh, man, I'm late again. C'mon, you guys, I gotta get going."

James poured the last of his whisky down his throat, while Billy left most of a beer untouched. "Drivin'," he smiled, although he had been drinking throughout the evening.

Reaching for his wallet, James asked, "Can you get the bill from Mad Dog so we can settle up?"

"No need," replied Billy. "He and I have an arrangement." Turning to Mad Dog, he called, "See ya later, man. We're outta here. Thanks!"

Mad Dog looked up from washing glasses at the bar, and called, "Good night, lads. Drive careful now, Billy."

The boy rolled his eyes and waved his hand at the man, as if pushing away his words. Mike and James said their goodnights to Mad Dog as the boys put on their jackets, and slipped out the back door.

It had been snowing since they had gone inside, and there was some frost on the windows of the car, too. Billy used the scraper to remove the frost, while Mike and James brushed off the snow with their hands.

Before long, the windows were clear and they were on their way.

On the ride home, James was thinking about how he felt. It had been a long time since he had enjoyed anything at all, and he had to admit, he'd had some fun with his mates that night. On the other hand, he also had to acknowledge that it was only after he started drinking, because the pain and rage about Angelina never left him, and were only tolerable if he drank.

Still, his evening out with his friends had proven to be a good idea, a nice change from hiding in his room. He decided he was going to have to do this more often.

There, alone in the dark, in the back seat of the car, music blasting from the front, he could have his thoughts to himself, and he let them wander to memories of his little sister. This was most unusual for him; he worked very hard at not thinking about her because it hurt too much, but for some reason, he could not help but remember the sweet little girl who used to sit on his bed, idolizing her oldest brother.

All of a sudden, thoughts of 'Pooh Sticks' rolled through his mind. When he and Angelina used to take their books and sit by the creek, sometimes they stood on the bridge and played 'Pooh Sticks', just like the characters in A.A. Milne's Winnie-the-Pooh books, which were among Angelina's favourites.

Together, they stood on the bridge, throwing their sticks down into the water, then running across to the other side of the bridge and cheering on their sticks, just like Pooh and his friends had done.

James was lost in thought; for the first time, he was having a happy memory of Angelina and it warmed his heart.

Angelina had been with James, on his bed, earlier that evening when his friends had come to call. She had worked very hard to try to send him a message about how he should really go out with them. She was thrilled when she heard him tell his friends 'yes', but she didn't know whether it was because she had been able to communicate with him, or if he would have done it anyway. It didn't much matter; the important thing was that he went!

She had stayed with her father after James left with his friends; Robert had been wandering through the house, restless and feeling unsettled. So after the boys left, Angelina decided to keep Daddy company for a while. She hovered near him as he paced, or while he stood, staring off into space. Concentrating as hard as she could, she whispered in his ear, telling him that she was there, that everything was okay, trying to comfort him. She scrunched up her face and with her eyes tightly squeezed shut, she did her very best to make him hear.

And just like with James, she was uncertain about whether or not Daddy heard her, but after a little while, he sat down and looked a little more calm.

Angelina's next stop was Kathy's room, and there she found her Mummy, hands resting on the arms of the rocking chair by the window, expressionless as she stared out at the moonlit snow. The Little Angel climbed up onto her mother's lap, and snuggled in like she used to do. She wished she could feel her mother's arms around her. But she could hear Mummy's heart beating slowly and steadily like before, and she loved the gentle rocking motion of that chair.

Angelina reached up and stroked her mother's face ever so gently, and trying as hard as she could, she did her best to say, "I love you, Mummy. I'm here."

This time, she was quite certain it worked. This time, Kathy looked almost startled. She brought up her hand and touched her face where Angelina had been stroking her, and wiped at it, as if it had tickled. Gone was the blank stare, and in its place was an intent look, as Kathy's eyes searched the room.

The Little Angel was still on her mother's lap, saying, "I'm here, Mummy! Right here!" She was thrilled! It seemed that she was finally beginning to get through, but she had not quite got there yet.

After a few moments, Kathy's face fell and she seemed very disappointed. Settling back into the chair, she resumed her rocking and staring, but she stopped now and then and gently laid her hand against her face, right where Angelina had touched it, as if she was wondering...

Angelina was elated! She was certain she had connected with her mother, and in her excitement, she thought it was worth another try with her brother.

The Little Angel found Elijah in his sister's bedroom with Frank that evening. It was awful the way the whole family just split apart and spent so much time alone; it shocked Angelina to see that this was how they lived after she crossed over to The Other Side.

When she found Elijah, he was telling her all about his first little while back at school. It had not been very long, but for the most part, he thought it was going fairly well. He told her that after that first awful day with Jimmy Watson, nothing really bad happened. People were whispering and pointing less and less, and he wasn't getting as many questions about how Angelina died, and had he seen her when she was dead, and what had she looked like, and was it creepy to have her die in the house, and was he scared of her ghost haunting them, and on and on like that.

He knew that this was all pretty difficult for children to absorb, and he did his best to remember that they simply did not understand, knowing that they were unaware that their questions might be upsetting for him. He was learning ways to answer, or not, and he was learning ways to change the subject or disappear when he'd had enough.

But the Jimmy Watson thing really did still bother him. He could not believe that even a kid could be so cruel. He was well aware that children can be really horrible to each other, but he was still stunned that a child could be so deliberately nasty. He wondered what the Head Master had said to Jimmy, or to his parents, and he wondered what the conversation had been between Jimmy and his Mum and Dad. He didn't know Jimmy's parents; he had no idea what kind of people they were, or how they might feel about their son being so horrible. They might be perfectly nice people who would be shocked to know what he said. Or maybe they were the kind of people who would laugh and think it was funny, although Elijah could not really believe that such adults existed.

Well, at least his teacher had given him a really big hug that day, and he felt like Angelina might have been there, too, and it was over now, so he was just carrying on, trying to get through each day, and put it further and further behind him.

These were the kinds of thoughts that he was sharing with Frank and with Angelina (though he was unaware that she was really there and listening), and it made him feel much better every time he did this.

On this particular evening, Elijah was sitting cross-legged on Angelina's bed, petting Frank who was curled up on the Raggedy Ann's chest, just like she used to do on Angelina's. Elijah was chattering away, telling Frank and

Angelina everything that was on his mind, when his little sister came and sat cross-legged, opposite him, staring him right in the face.

Elijah kept talking, and Angelina was really concentrating, hoping he would see her, hoping he would know she was there. She had been trying with her whole family that night, and was getting a little tuckered out, but still, she focused as she had been taught, and prayed that Elijah would see her.

'After all', she thought, 'Elijah is the most receptive of all of them. I shouldn't have to work as hard with him as I do with the others.'

Her efforts were not entirely successful, but Elijah stopped mid-sentence, and started to look around the room, as if he was searching for something, just as his mother had done. He could not see his sister, but she was sure that for the first time, he was certain that she was there with him.

Angelina was very excited! She started bouncing up and down, saying, "I'm here! I'm here, Elijah! Look! Right in front of you!!" But her words did not get through.

That was okay. She realized that she was at least beginning to make a bit of a connection with each of her family members, and she hoped that someday, they would all be open to communicating with her. Her Teachers had told her that it did not always work, and certainly not with every person. People have to be open to it, and that, in itself, takes a lot of particular circumstances to exist at once.

Later that night, after spending time with her parents and Elijah, Angelina decided to drop in on James and see what was happening for him. It was when he was in the back of the car on the way home, music blasting from the front seat. She crawled up onto James's lap, and started thinking about when they used to go and read at the creek. Quite often, they read Winnie-the-Pooh stories, which she had so loved. James had long ago admitted to her that he loved them, too, but he swore her to secrecy; no one must know! Angelina had giggled that day, and promised her big brother that she would never tell.

Even if he had ever been bored with her little girl games and stories, James never, ever let her see it. She always felt so special with him; he made her feel loved and important.

And there, in the back of Billy's car, Angelina had to let James know how loved and important he was, too. Remembering how they played 'Pooh Sticks', she sent the memories to him, in hopes that he would receive them, and that he would understand the message behind them.

In the moonlight, Angelina thought she saw the faintest little curl in the corners of James's mouth, possibly indicating a hint of a smile, while a quiet tear softly rolled down his cheek, and she thought maybe, oh, just maybe he understood.

Seven

It was April. James's 16th birthday was approaching. But no one had discussed a celebration with him. Once again, he felt himself becoming angry with Angelina for having turned their lives upside down, then was immediately even more angry with himself for having felt that way. This was supposed to have been a big deal, a major event in his life. He had been looking forward to it for years, believing it was almost like being an adult.

He wondered whether his family was planning to ignore it entirely, because Angelina had been born on the same date. Feeling angry and defensive, he did not want to bring it up with them; he wanted to wait and see what happened, and if they missed it, he was going to enjoy punishing them. Elijah might mess that up for him; that kid was not likely to forget his brother's birthday, and would probably insist that their parents do something to acknowledge it, letting them off the hook and not allowing him the chance to hurt them in return for the countless ways in which they had hurt him.

He was making plans of his own anyway, since there did not seem to be any others in the works. He was going to Mad Dog's with Mike and Billy. They had taken to spending an awful lot of time there in the past couple of months, and often, Billy and Mad Dog had those strange little private 'chats' but neither said a word about them. That is, not until recently, when James finally decided to voice his opinions, and confronted Billy with what he thought was the truth.

And as it turned out, he was right. Billy was running drugs for Mad Dog, which was why the boys got free drinks; they bought the boys' silence. I mean, how many underage boys got to drink in a pub? And at no cost to them whatsoever? It was a mutually agreeable arrangement, plus Billy earned a decent amount of cash from the deals. And what young man with a car can't use lots of money?

Billy had been reluctant to say anything to his friends, just in case he or Mad Dog ever got caught. He wanted to keep them out of trouble, but one night after he had exchanged cash for more drugs with Mad Dog behind the bar, James confronted him when he sat back down with his friends.

It had been kind of funny, really, wild boy Billy trying to protect James and Mike. Usually, he was the one trying to get them into trouble, not keep them out of it! But maybe he had decided that legal trouble was a bit more than his friends needed.

After James opened the can of worms, and Billy let them all out, Mike asked, "So what kind of drugs are we talkin' about here, mate?"

"Pretty much anything you want," replied Billy. "This is a pub. Lots of people come in here. I can get anything somebody wants. Why? You interested?" he asked, quite surprised.

"Yeah, maybe. I dunno. Things are getting pretty bad at home. Since my dad split, my mom's been making my brothers and me nuts. She's a mess, and dad hardly ever comes around. They fight on the phone all the time. Whenever we talk to either of them, it's like they're trying to get us to take sides, and they're using us to hurt each other, too. I'm pretty sick of the whole mess, and I'm thinkin' I could stand to feel a little better now and then."

"Yeah, I know what you mean," said James. "That's why I started drinking after -- well, when I didn't want to feel things any more. So what can you get us, Billy? Do you have anything on you right now?"

"Sure, mate, got some weed just now, and Mad Dog never minds if I use a bit myself. Wanna smoke a joint?"

Mike and James looked at each other, and no one seemed to come up with a reason why they shouldn't give it a whirl, so they both replied, "Sure!" and gathered in tighter while Billy took out a cigarette paper and a plastic bag filled with marijuana, and created what appeared to be an expertly rolled joint.

Stuffing the materials back in his pocket, he motioned with his head toward the back door. As the three passed the bar, Billy called out to Mad Dog, "Back in a sec, just gonna be out back," and gave him a wink. Mad Dog nodded in reply, and turned back to wiping the bar.

Once out in the cool spring evening, the three boys huddled together with anticipation and excitement, smoking the joint quickly. Before the last of it was gone, they were already feeling the effects of the drug. Laughing, they retreated to their little back room with the pool table, and ordered another round of drinks.

James had thoroughly enjoyed the feeling that he got from alcohol, although it did tend to make him more angry than he was without it, but smoking a joint was even better, as far as he was concerned. He found that it calmed him, made him care a lot less about his troubles. A pleasant change, he thought. And this is how he had spent much of his time with Mike and Billy ever since, coming home late, and often missing school. It had not been that long since he had returned to classes; his father and the school really had to fight with him to get him to go back and finally, he relented, although it was mostly because he could no longer stand being in the house with his mother the way she was.

His rage and his attitude kept anyone from bothering him with stupid questions - or any questions, for that matter. He rolled into school late when he felt like it, and before long, was not showing up for classes on an increasingly frequent basis as well. Sometimes, when he was meant to be in class, he was found, instead, smoking outside the school, having picked up yet another bad habit. He was not at all bothered by the fact that he had been given homework that he had no intention of completing, or by the threat of suspension or even expulsion. He figured he would just do what he wanted, and if that included spending the odd class or day on his own, then tough luck. His parents and teachers would just have to suck it up.

Robert was usually the one to talk to the staff at the school. If the phone rang while he was at work, Kathy rarely answered it any more, happy to have voice mail take messages. There was the occasional morning when Kathy thought she might be feeling a little better, and Elijah always knew it was one of those days because his mother would appear in the kitchen before he went to school. It didn't happen often, or if he saw her at all, she was stumbling around in her dressing gown, looking for coffee and barely mumbling

"Good morning" to him before heading back up to her room.

Elijah was beginning to think that his family was never going to be all right again. It had been three and a half months since Angelina died, and it seemed that everyone was just stuck and unable to move away from that terrible time. Maybe there was more that he could do, though he was not sure what that might be. There were only a couple of things he did know for certain: he felt much better when he talked to his sister, and things in the family were not improving yet. In fact, he was pretty sure that they were getting worse.

Alone in his sister's room, Elijah noticed the calendar on the wall above the bed, still showing last December, with a basket of kittens wearing Father Christmas hats pictured above the month. His mother still refused to allow anything to change in that room, but Elijah decided it was time. Chances were she might not notice anyway; she did not seem to notice much of anything any more. Ensuring that the door was tightly closed, and feeling just a little nervous, Elijah went to the basket of untouched Christmas gifts and took out the new ‘Kitten calender’, which Kathy had bought for Angelina, something she had done every Christmas since the girl loved cats so much.

Climbing on the bed, Elijah took down the old calendar, staring wistfully at December 25th for a while before carefully closing it, and laying it gently on the desk. He picked up the new one, and opened it to April. Hanging it on the nail, he stood back to see how it looked. For months, he had been staring at the December kittens in Father Christmas hats and now, there was an adorable picture of kittens playing amongst some brightly coloured flowers.

In a way, it was sad for Elijah to see the new picture; he had grown accustomed to seeing December, and the dates before Angelina died. It was almost like he could pretend it was one of those days when he hid himself away in her room.

But on the other hand, Elijah well knew that it was time this family moved ahead. Although it might feel as though they were being disloyal to Angelina, or as if they were forgetting her, he knew that it was not the case. He knew they had to move on with their lives, that it was what Angelina would want for them. It was the right thing to do, but he was the only one who recognized it.

Elijah picked up the old calendar from Angelina's desk, and a plastic container of crayons. Removing a gold one, he drew a simple angel shape around December 25th, a head, halo, wings and long gown. Then saying goodbye to the past, Elijah respectfully closed the calendar and taking great care not to bend it, put it away in one of Angelina's dresser drawers.

Settling back onto the bed, Elijah had a look at the new calendar. Staring at the month of April, it suddenly occurred to him that it was almost James's birthday, but he had not heard anyone in the house mention it. And he was certain he knew why. Angelina had been born on James's 11th birthday. She would have been five years old pretty soon. How awful for James to have to share every birthday forever with the haunting memory of their dead sister!

Elijah hoped that this birthday could be made very special for James. He was worried about whether or not his parents would be willing but he had to try. He was pretty sure he could get Dad to go along with it, but Mum...well, he wasn't too sure about her at all.

That night, Robert came home just before Elijah went to bed. The boy was in his pajamas, having just got out of the bath, and he was in his room, towel-drying his hair. He heard Robert coming up the stairs, and was happy to see that his father poked his head in when passing Elijah's room.

"Hey, how's it going?" Robert asked, as cheerfully as possible.

"Hey, Dad. Not bad," was Elijah's quiet reply.

"School okay?"

Why was it that was always the first thing grown-ups asked? When was his dad going to ask how he really was, or something else that was more meaningful??

Elijah sighed and said, "Fine, Dad."

Wanting Robert to come in and talk, but unsure how to ask, he wished that his father could just *know* that his son needed him. "Dad?"

"Yes?"

Elijah was stuck. What next? What should he say? All he could say was nothing.

"What's the matter, Son?" asked Robert.

"Well, I -- I wanted to talk to you," was the stilted reply.

Robert came in and sat down on Elijah's bed, patting the space next to him. "Come here, Son. Tell me what's on your mind."

It had been such a long time since Elijah had seen his dad be so -- so normal. The boy went and sat beside his father, then stared at the floor, not having any idea how to begin.

Robert was patient, and gave the boy some time to collect his thoughts. It had been a long time since any member of this family had really spoken to the others; they were all out of practice, and Elijah's uncomfortable silence really brought the point home.

"Well, Dad, it's about -- it's about, um..." He took a deep breath and tried again, the words coming out in a rush. "It's about James's birthday, Dad. No one's mentioned it, and I think it's because it was Angelina's birthday, too."

Robert was quiet for a moment, remembering the day Angelina was born. He sighed heavily, contemplating what Kathy might say about the subject.

"Yes, Elijah. I was thinking about it recently myself. I'm not quite sure what to do about it. James has retreated from the family so much; he's going to school less and less, he's out almost every night, coming in late. I don't know what he's doing, but I fear he's up to no good; he's become so secretive. I don't even know if he wants us to celebrate his birthday," Robert said sadly, as he hung his head.

"Yes, Dad, of course he does! I know it!"

"Has he said anything to you?" asked Robert, raising his eyebrows, hopefully surprised at the idea that James had actually spoken to anyone about anything of some significance.

"Well, no, but I do know that this family is really in trouble, Dad." Elijah was a bit shocked that he had allowed the words to fall out of his mouth; he had not even known that he was going to say them. And having started, they seemed to keep coming. "We have to move on. We can't keep going like this. It's wrong, Dad. Angelina would hate to see what we've become! We have to start somewhere, and it might as well be with James's birthday!"

At the same time relieved and afraid, Elijah stood waiting for his father's response. At first, there wasn't one. Robert just stared at the wall across the room, with a faraway look in his eyes.

Finally, he spoke. "You're right, Elijah. I don't know how to start. I don't know how to fix this. I don't know how to help James. But you're right. We have to start somewhere. What do you think we should do?"

Elijah was thrilled that his father had heard him and agreed with his thoughts. The boy's relief was easily visible in his body and on his face.

"I don't know, Dad. I feel like I don't know James at all any more, but I was thinking, maybe we can reach him with something from the past. Maybe we could plan a surprise picnic at the creek in the woods behind the house. He has always loved to spend so much time there."

Robert pondered Elijah's idea. "Yes, I know he used to love it there, but he used to spend so much time there with Angelina. Maybe it will upset him."

"I know, Dad. But we can't keep pretending Angelina never lived. We're not allowed to talk about her. We're supposed to act like she was never part of our family. She and James were born on the same date, and he's going to have to get used to thinking about that on every one of his birthdays for the rest of his life!"

Robert thought for a moment, knowing that Elijah was absolutely right. He agreed with almost everything the boy said. "I'll think about it, and talk to your Mum. Thanks, Elijah. It's time someone said it, and it should have been one of the parents in the house, not you. Although I have to say, I think doing something at the creek might do more harm than good."

There was so much more he wanted to say, but he didn't know where to start, and he was already feeling rather overwhelmed by Elijah's words.

"Maybe you and I should plan this, Dad. Maybe you shouldn't bother Mum with it, except to tell her that we think we need to do this," suggested the boy. "And you may be right about the creek, Dad. It was just a thought, but as long as we celebrate in some way, I think that's what's important."

Robert nodded slowly. "Yes, I think you're right. Okay. For now, it'll just be the two of us making plans. You had better try and get some sleep now, and we'll talk again tomorrow. Thanks, Elijah."

As the boy climbed into bed, he stopped for a hug from his father before settling in under the blankets. It was his first in a long time and almost made him cry. Snapping off the light and closing the door as he left the room, it almost made Robert cry, too.

Although Elijah felt some relief and some hope about the state of his family, there was still a sense of uneasiness gnawing at him. He lay awake for a long time before finally falling into a restless sleep filled with anxious dreams.

Angelina had been watching as Elijah decided it was time to change the calendar in her bedroom. She was with him as he realized that someone in the family needed to do something to start moving these people forward. Watching her parents and her brothers since her death, she had been having many discussions with her Teachers about her family's struggles. While the Little Angel was learning and adjusting on The Other Side, her family was meant to be learning and adjusting as well. But it was not going very well at all.

Angelina was very excited when she saw Elijah take down the calendar and put up the new one, and it was a bittersweet moment when he drew the gold angel around the date that she left her physical body before putting the calendar away. She was happy to see that the first step had been taken toward healing, and although the family had a very long and difficult road ahead, it gave her hope.

What she did not know, however, was that things were going to get a lot worse before they got any better.

Eight

It was late morning when Kathy rolled out of bed. This had been the normal course since Angelina died, except for a little while when Elijah first went back to school, and Kathy was trying to make an effort to return to her life as a mother. But that had not lasted very long. By the time Kathy arose on weekdays, Robert was long since gone to work, Elijah was in school, and she was never certain where James was if he wasn't in his bed.

Every day began as a thick fog, a hangover from the sleeping pills that she had been taking for some time. Robert was unaware of the fact that Kathy had spoken with her doctor not long after Angelina died and she had been given the sleeping pills plus extra tranquilizers, about which Robert knew nothing.

Many mornings, Kathy thought she could get through the day without a pill; there was some part of her that was beginning to consider the notion that she may have a problem. But she never had to be up and around very long before she started to feel too much, preferring, instead, the numbing effect of her pills. Defending her decision, she would always tell herself that it was just too soon. After all, her four-year-old child had died. How was she just supposed to get on with her life right away?

She had got very good at giving herself excuses and 'reasons' to continue living on pills, and she had even managed to convince herself that her reason for not telling Robert about most of them was because she didn't want him to worry about her. But of course, it was really because something inside her knew that this was wrong, that she had a problem. She was afraid that she would not be able to hide it and that Robert would make her stop taking the pills. There was no way that she could face that.

Kathy dragged herself out of bed, and putting on a dressing gown, she went and ran a bath. It was a beautiful spring day; the sun poured in through the windows and for the first time that year, she noticed how dirty they were. She would have to get round to cleaning them, she told herself, realizing there were many long-neglected chores waiting for her.

There was a frightening stack of paper sitting on her desk. She knew that much of it was made up of sympathy cards and letters, and the idea of facing those and answering them was still too much to bear. She could not believe that it was almost four months since her beloved daughter had died; it felt like it was just last week. Some part of her knew that she should be trying to put her life back together, yet every time such a thought crossed her mind, she felt disloyal to Angelina. She simply could not imagine moving on with her life. It would be like forgetting that Angelina had ever lived.

In fact, rather than forgetting she lived, Kathy wanted to remember every second of her life, and although she had been burying herself in a haze of drugs, she was well aware that Angelina's birthday was just days away. She was struggling to imagine getting through that day, and she was certain that it was going to be even harder because of having to try to look happy, celebrating James's birthday. To her, this would only emphasize the fact that Angelina was dead. She did not need her nose rubbed in it, and although James would be expecting a celebration, surely he could understand if they did not have one this year. Besides, he had been almost completely antisocial since Angelina's death; Kathy allowed herself to believe that James would prefer his birthday go unnoticed and ignored.

As sometimes happened when she first awoke, Kathy thought that maybe this would be a day that she could manage without a pill. At least for a while. And she thought maybe she could manage to do something around the house or for the family that day; she was willing to try.

Slipping into the hot bath, she tried to be positive about the rest of the day, wanting to see if she could take any little step toward having a normal life, as long as it did not mean letting go of Angelina. She wasn't sure how that would work; life would never be normal again because her daughter was dead. But something told her she should at least try to figure it out.

By the time Kathy had finished bathing and was dressed, the sleeping pill fog had cleared somewhat and she was looking forward to her coffee. As she pulled out the coffee maker and filled the pot with water, she saw a note from Robert, saying that he would try to be home a little earlier that evening. It was simply signed with an "R"; no words of love, no "xox" like he used to do.

'Well,' she thought, 'maybe he was just in a hurry this morning.' Although when she stopped to think about it, she didn't feel particularly loving towards Robert, so she should not be surprised that it might be the same for him towards her. It's not that he had done anything wrong; it was just that from the moment Angelina had died in her arms, all emotions except grief had been shut off. She knew in her head that she still loved her husband and her sons, but she could not, for the life of her, connect with those feelings at all.

And although this probably should have worried her, at that particular time, it did not. She believed that she merely needed more time.

Blinking against the bright sunlight, Kathy looked out at the garden, remembering how Angelina loved to help with planting and watering, or even with weed-pulling. She gazed out at the places where the two of them had planted annuals each spring, places which were, of course, awaiting new flowers.

Angelina had looked so adorable with a big floppy hat and oversized children's sunglasses, digging away in the dirt and being, oh, so excited when she was allowed to take one of the 'babies', as she called the little plants, and put them into the ground. She especially loved the watering afterward, but tended to become rather mud-covered by the end of it.

Lost in her memories for a while, Kathy thought that it might be a good idea to go and work in the garden that day; maybe she would feel closer to Angelina. Spurred on by that prospect, while the coffee was brewing, Kathy went and changed into clothes that were more appropriate for digging and getting dirty outside.

Before long, there she was, cup in hand, actually going outside to work in the garden. She was quite proud of herself and thought that this would be perfect; an attempt to be normal without leaving Angelina behind.

Kathy went to the shed, and brought out a bucket of hand tools for digging, weeding and so on. She found rubbish sacks and plant pots, all kinds of things that she would be needing. Without having made a trip to the garden center yet, there was nothing to plant, but there was much work to be done in preparation anyway.

Finding gardening gloves, Kathy eagerly put them on and set to work, digging out weeds, and removing all the dead branches and leaves from the previous year. She kept seeing her Little Angel right there beside her, and in a matter of minutes, found herself talking to the child.

"Oh, my Angel, do you remember when we worked out here the past couple of years? Even when you were just a very wee tot, you loved to help in whatever ways you could. How I wish you were here with me now! You could help me with all of this digging and we could talk and play at the same time, just like before!"

And with that, Kathy started to chatter to herself, as if Angelina were really there, too.

After a couple of hours, Kathy was stunned to look around and see how much she had accomplished. She felt a little silly pretending that Angelina had been with her, but decided that since no one had to know, it shouldn't be a big deal. She was certain that she was not the first mother to imagine such a thing, and it had made her feel so much better, what could be the harm?

By the time she had put all the weeds into rubbish sacks, and had tidied up all the gardening tools, it was well into the afternoon. It was so easy for the day to escape when it didn't really begin until at least noon.

Kathy had really enjoyed 'playing with Angelina', and while still lost in thought, feeling as though she was with her little girl, she headed upstairs to shower and change into clean clothes. Passing Angelina's bedroom, she glanced inside and caught a glimpse of the basket full of Christmas gifts which had never been used.

Instantly, the grieving mother felt as though she had been slammed in the stomach with a bag of bricks. The reality of Angelina's death came rushing back full force, and it felt as though it had just happened in that moment. Kathy threw herself onto her daughter's bed, curling up with the Raggedy Ann and sobbing until she could cry no more.

Lying still and quiet, Kathy's eyes drifted around the room. Everything was as Angelina had left it, except that the bed had been made and the Christmas gifts had been brought upstairs and left untouched. There were her Christmas Eve clothes, draped over the back of the chair. Kathy had put them there after Angelina had gone to bed for the last time.

In the corner, standing on a table was a beautiful doll house that Robert had made for her when she was a baby. All the furniture and the little people were exactly where Angelina had left them. Kathy dusted a little around them, but did not want to touch them, so the doll house was looking like it could use a good cleaning. It was the same with everything else in Angelina's room. All her little toys and things on her desk or shelves, anything that she had touched was to be left exactly where it had been the last time their Little Angel had used it. In this way, Kathy felt that they were still connected to her; they didn't have to say goodbye, not really.

Her eyes continued to drift through the room, and eventually, found their way to the calendar above the bed. Expecting to see the kittens with the Father Christmas hats, it was a monumental shock when instead, she saw that someone had taken down that calendar, and had replaced it with the current one! She was irate! Absolutely livid! She could not imagine which of the other three family members in the house could have done this, or why. And just where was the other calendar?

She leapt up from the bed and began searching Angelina's room, trying not to disturb anything, but carefully thumbing through the books and papers on the shelves, and going through the desk and dresser drawers. And finally, there it was. She had found the previous year's calendar. Quickly opening it to the last page, December, she was stunned to find the little gold angel drawn around the 25th.

Kathy would have been no more shocked if someone had dumped a bucket of ice water on her head at that moment. She'd had such a wonderful afternoon, feeling as though Angelina was still here, still alive, still a part of the family, and suddenly, she was thrown back into having to remember that her little girl was dead.

Afraid that the next step might be to remove the calendar from Angelina's room altogether, Kathy took it to her own room, and hid it under some little-used clothing in one of her drawers. And immediately afterward, she went to the medicine cabinet and found her pills.

The Little Angel had been watching her mother that day. At first, she was very excited to see that Mummy was going to go and work in the garden; she thought that it meant she was getting better. Her Teachers had been telling her some of the ways in which her mother might demonstrate that she was accepting Angelina's death and carrying on with her own life again, and this seemed a very good start, indeed.

But as time passed, the Little Angel heard her mother say things that did not sit well with the little girl. Though she was very new at Life on The Other Side, she knew enough to realize that her mother might even be getting worse.

Angelina had listened carefully to her mother's words as she tended to the garden. When she could no longer stand it, she went to one of her Teachers, deeply disturbed about what she had witnessed.

"Teacher!" cried the Little Angel. "I need your help! I am confused by what I am seeing in my mother and I am not sure if I'm right in thinking that she's not doing very well."

"What is it, Angelina? What is it about your mother that is troubling you so?" asked the Teacher, kneeling down to face the Little Angel.

"Well, I have been learning about so many things since I came here, and one of them is about accepting that it happened. Not only must I accept it, but those I left behind must, as well. You and my other Teachers have told me much about this, because it is one of the hardest lessons. And I have been paying very close attention and trying really hard to learn."

"Yes, Angelina, you have been a diligent little student, and you are doing very well," remarked the Teacher.

But the Little Angel was too concerned about her mother to acknowledge the praise, and she continued. "Well, today, I was very excited to see my mother going outside to work on the garden. She has been stuck in the house, and mostly in her bedroom since I left, and she has been unable to accept that I needed to be here and not there. Today, I thought she was taking a step away from that life, and toward accepting my physical death."

The Little Angel paused, a little furrow in her brow, uncertain about how to explain what was troubling her. At last, she was ready to try.

"You know how you have said that it's good when people talk to us after we've come here?" she queried.

"Yes, Angelina, of course. It helps them feel closer to us, and especially when they believe that we can really hear them," replied the Teacher.

"Well, Mama was talking to me today. And at first I thought it was good. She was out in the garden, doing something besides hiding in her room, and she was talking to me. I was so excited, Teacher. I thought she was beginning to accept what happened.

"But then..." The Little Angel wore an expression of worry as she took a deep breath and let out a long sigh. After a moment, she tried once again to explain what was bothering her.

"When Elijah talks to me, I know that he's okay. Well, I mean, I know that he is sad and he misses me, and I know that he's having troubles because of the mess my family is in, but I mean, he's okay about me being here while they are all over there.

"Elijah talks to me like I'm here. But Mummy talked to me today like I'm there. And it was really creepy, Teacher. I don't know how else to explain it. She was talking to me about helping her in the garden. She was asking me to hand things to her, and saying 'thank you' as if I'd done it. She wasn't talking to me like she knows I'm here. She was playing 'Let's Pretend', and I don't think that's good, is it, Teacher?"

Angelina looked up at her Teacher, her big blue eyes filled with concern for her Mummy, in a way, hoping that she got it right because she knew that would mean she was learning her lessons on The Other Side, but in another way, hoping that she was wrong, because she didn't want to see her Mummy getting any worse.

The Teacher smiled down at the Little Angel. "Yes, my dear, you are right. Your Mummy was playing 'Let's Pretend.' And you are also right that it's not good. Your Mummy simply cannot let go of you yet; she has not accepted the fact that you are meant to be here now, and she is afraid that if she accepts it, that will mean she is being disloyal to you. She is afraid that if she lets go and moves on without you in her everyday life, it will be like leaving you behind, like forgetting that you ever lived. She does not realize that you are still with her and the rest of your family, it's just in a different way. And she does not realize that nothing will make her forget you, not time, not distance, not death.

"And she was also doing it because she misses you, Angelina. It's that simple.

"It's one thing when people talk to us as if we are dead and they know it, but it's very unhealthy when they refuse to accept that fact and pretend that we are still alive.

"Good for you, Angelina. You are learning your lessons very well. And try not to worry too much about your Mummy. She will learn in time; she will have to. You will see; certain things are going to happen in your family and she will have no choice."

The Little Angel thought that this sounded rather ominous, and was not certain that she wanted to know what the Teacher meant. Preferring to leave the conversation where it ended, she thanked her Teacher and went off to be alone and to think about all of this for a while.

Kathy had been grateful when her tranquilizer took effect and she was considerably more numb than she had been in Angelina's room earlier. She had gone to bed for a while, and although she heard Elijah come in from school, she did not feel prepared to speak with him or anyone else. She was uncertain about how she should approach the issue of the calendar in Angelina's room, and needed a little time to pull herself together after being so terribly upset that afternoon.

Telling herself that she would see him later, she ignored the sounds of her son, finding a drink and a snack, and settling in after a day at school. She drifted off to sleep for a while, restless and unhappy.

Kathy was awakened by the sound of a soft tapping at the door, seemingly only minutes later, but really, it was a couple of hours. The sun had not yet set, although it would not be long. Her head felt thick and full of cotton; her throat was tight and dry.

Another knock, and then Robert's voice. "Kathy? Are you awake?" he asked, gently.

"Mm-hmm," was the only reply his wife could manage. Blinking as she sat up, she saw her husband come in and close the door behind him. Crossing the room, he sat on the bed next to her.

"How are you, Kath?" he asked, real concern in his voice.

A blank stare was all he got in response.

"Not so good, I guess," he answered for her. "Well, dinner's just about ready. Elijah and I need to talk to you, so can you please come down and eat with us? We hardly ever see you at the table and we miss you, Kath." Robert reached over and put his hand on his wife's arm.

His little show of affection was jarring for Kathy. Prior to Angelina's death, she had been a very openly affectionate woman, but she could not cope with such displays any more; they pushed her to feel, and this was unacceptable. She pulled her arm away as she threw back the blankets and got out of bed, not wanting him to know that she was avoiding his touch. But it was too late. He was used to her moving away in one form or another, every time he touched her at all. A heavy sigh escaped his lips as he hung his head and turned away.

"Yes, okay, Robert. Let me have a few minutes to collect myself and I'll be down," said his wife, sounding more weary than usual.

Rising from the bed, Robert walked across the room and with his hand on the doorknob, he hesitated momentarily, as if he was going to say something. Apparently thinking better of it, he opened the door and left, closing it behind him.

Sounds of his retreating footsteps floated through the bedroom, his unspoken words hanging thick and heavy. Kathy wondered what it was that he and Elijah wanted to discuss. Well, she had something to discuss, too, although she wasn't certain when or how she would do it. She was fairly certain that no one in the family was going to appreciate how she felt about the calendar issue.

Brushing her teeth and washing her face helped her to feel a little more awake. Running her fingers through her hair, she tried to make it look a little more presentable, then prepared to face her family in the kitchen.

Robert had set the table for the meal that Elijah had prepared. At ten years old, the lad had become quite an extraordinary helper in the past few months. With the passing weeks, he had seen how many chores were not being looked after, and in his effort to help his family to cope with losing Angelina, he had realized that there was much he could do to make a difference.

He had been preparing meals, doing the washing up, taking care of most of the laundry, and cleaning the house as best he could, taking on more and more responsibility the longer his mother had been unable to manage her usual duties. Much of what he did went unnoticed. With Robert being gone so much of every day, he paid very little attention to the household tasks, unless they were long overdue and hard to ignore.

And Kathy did not seem to notice whether anything was done, or needed doing; so preoccupied was she. James - well, he managed to look after his own laundry, as he had been doing for some time. And other than that, no one saw much of him any more. He certainly was not involved with the family or the running of their home. He popped in, grabbed something from the fridge now and then, locked himself in his room for a while, or on rare occasion, actually ate with one or more of his family members, but always in silence; he had very little to say.

Kathy entered the kitchen and saw the table set for four. Another of those sights that was like a knife in her heart, another little reminder that Angelina was dead. She was so sick of having it put in her face all the time.

The kitchen was filled with a wonderful aroma. She had got used to Elijah cooking and was enjoying not having to bother with it any more. "It smells great in here, Eli. What did you make?"

"I used some leftover stuff and made a Chinese chicken casserole with some rice. I put lots of pineapple in the casserole, Mum, because I know you like it." Elijah was desperate for his mother's approval and a little recognition, the little boy in him begging for some attention, the wise and spiritual part of him taking a back seat for a while.

"You're really good to us, Elijah. You're becoming quite an amazing chef at a tender age. I know I haven't told you nearly enough how much I appreciate all your help around here. I'm a very lucky Mum to have such a great kid who doesn't mind taking over for a while. Thank you." And giving him a most sincere look, she got quite choked up, and dared not say another word for fear of coming apart entirely.

What Elijah really wanted at that moment was a hug. But he remembered his first day back to school in January, and he could see by the look on his mother's face that she was already feeling emotional enough, and a hug would not be a good idea. He desperately missed the warm and affectionate woman she used to be; he longed for her to return.

Well, he couldn't think about that just then. At least he could be glad that she had been noticing all he had been doing. And for him, right at that moment, that was about as good as noticing *him*.

"Dinner's ready, if you and Dad want to sit down. I don't know where James is, but we might as well start without him," said Elijah. 'As usual,' he added to himself.

Once they were all seated, and the food was being passed around, the room was filled with an awkward silence. It seemed as though everyone had something to say, yet no one really wanted to speak.

Finally, it was Robert who began the conversation. "Kath, there's something we need to talk about, and I know it's going to be difficult, but we haven't much choice."

Her stomach did a little flip and she replied, "With a preamble like that, I can't wait to hear the rest," the sarcasm quite evident in her voice.

Elijah and Robert looked at each other and then at Kathy. This time, it was Elijah who spoke. He was not even planning to say anything, but suddenly, he found words spilling out of his mouth, despite the warning voice in his head yelling at him to stop.

"Mummy, it's going to be James's birthday in a few days, and no one has mentioned anything about it. And it's his 16th. It's extra special. We can't just let it pass by and ignore it!" He hoped his pleading manner would get through to his mother. And he hoped she did not get angry with him for having brought up 'The Subject' without really having said anything specific.

Kathy was silent for several seconds. Robert was giving her time to absorb what Elijah had said before trying to elicit an opinion from her.

Well, there it was. She had been hoping to sail right past this upcoming date without having to acknowledge it, but apparently, that was not meant to be. And now that it was put in her lap, she did not know what to do with it. Her mind was racing with thoughts of Angelina, and previous birthday parties for both her and James. And it was racing with fearful thoughts about trying to get through a party for James while not having one for Angelina, yet again shoving her death down Kathy's throat.

She also knew that if she did not soon make an effort to put her life together, she was going to get increasing pressure from Robert to see a therapist. She was going to have to get through this, and suddenly, an idea came to her. And she was sure that her plan was going to make a world of difference. She thought she would be all right after all, as long as she said nothing about her idea.

"Yes. I agree. We must do something to celebrate James's special day. Does either of you have any idea about what we should do?"

Elijah and Robert were speechless. Neither had expected such a response. They were prepared only for Kathy to rebel, to become emotional, to be upset. Could it be that she was getting better? Could it be that she was going to be all right again soon?

Excitedly, the two began discussing ideas, and as their eager conversation filled the kitchen, Kathy sat smiling, appearing to be listening, but she was making plans of her own.

Nine

Friday night, James had come in very late, long after the rest of the family was asleep, having had plenty to drink, and having smoked a couple of joints as well. It was actually the wee hours of Saturday morning when he stumbled into Angelina's room on the way to his own, and closing the door behind him, he wished her a happy birthday, and wished one for himself as well.

He was angry, as always, and furious that the little girl could not have lived to see many more. It was just wrong that a child couldn't make it to five years old. Good grief, she didn't even get to start school. What kind of cruelty is that??

And he was not looking forward to his own birthday always reminding him of her death. They should have been celebrating together until they were old prunes. This was just WRONG and the whole idea added fuel to a fire that was already raging out of control.

James lay down on Angelina's bed, as he often did late at night, waking Frank from a sound sleep on the Raggedy Ann's chest. The sad young man curled up with both the cat and the doll, and cried himself to sleep.

Elijah had been lying awake for much of that Friday night. Saturday was going to be a difficult day full of mixed emotions, and the sensitive boy could not help but be affected by contemplating what lay ahead. He had heard James coming in and going to Angelina's room in the early morning hours, followed by the quiet sobs on the other side of his bedroom wall as his brother fell asleep in the little girl's room.

He tossed and turned, unable to get comfortable or to stop the anxious and unsettling thoughts that were rolling through his head. As dawn approached, Elijah knew it was going to be a very long day, and before it began, he was already wishing it was over.

Robert was asleep when he rolled over and unconsciously put his arm around his wife and snuggled in behind her. Kathy, however, had been very much awake at that point, and she froze, unsure about what to do next. In part, she missed the comfort and warmth of her husband's embrace. She longed to lean on him again, to fall apart and cry while he held her. Prior to Angelina's death, they had always been so close and had relied on each other through everything.

But this was different. And Kathy feared that if she let down her guard, if she let herself cry in his arms, she might shatter into a million pieces and never be whole again. Lying there in the faint, early morning light, Robert's breath warm on the back of her neck as he slept, the world seemed safe and peaceful, and just for a moment, Kathy could forget that her sweet daughter was dead. Just for a moment, she allowed herself to believe that they were all fine and well, and that there was no big, horrible thing hanging over their lives, crushing them to death.

A few bittersweet tears rolled down Kathy's face, and came to rest on her pillow. She held Robert's arm a little tighter, and ever so slightly moved her body just a wee bit closer to him, carefully, so as not to wake him. He must not know; she dared not let him see her be so vulnerable.

And after a little while, she drifted off.

Robert woke some time later, and finding himself wrapped around his sleeping wife, instantly disentangled himself from her, afraid that if she woke, she would be upset with him for being so close. He ached for them to return to the way they used to be. They had enjoyed such a wonderful marriage; they always supported one another, talked to each other, were very physically affectionate with one another. This thick and tall defensive wall that his wife had erected absolutely terrified Robert. He had no idea what to do about it, how to get round it, how to get over it, under it or through it. He kept hoping that in time, she would break it down herself.

But in the meantime, he just kept putting one foot in front of the other, always trying to be respectful of whatever it was she needed -- or didn't -- from him.

It was time to get up and get on with the difficult day. Saturday, James's birthday. And Angelina's, too. Carefully, rolling out of bed so as not to disturb

Kathy, Robert sighed heavily and headed for the shower. As he stood under the slightly cool spray, he thought back to James's arrival into the world. Kathy had endured a long, hard labour, their baby obviously not in a rush to make an appearance.

And finally, there he was. Their firstborn child, a healthy nine and a half pounds, squealing and sucking on his fist, ready to take on the world.

Then there was the trauma of Elijah's birth, after that violent accident. Weighing in at just over three pounds, and with some respiratory problems and other concerns, it was a scary time for the family, doubtful that Kathy would survive and it had not looked too promising for Elijah either.

And after all they had been through with Kathy's long and difficult recovery from the accident, after all those heart-breaking disappointments with the miscarriages, there was the miracle of their Little Angel. She was truly Heaven sent, and although they were devastated when they learned that she was a very ill baby, they always appreciated the time they had with their sweet daughter. She had hardly taken any time at all to come screaming into the world, announcing her arrival, a strength of spirit belying her physical condition.

It was such a shock, such a terrible shock to find out that they may only have a little bit of time with their sweet Little Angel, and they did all they could to give her a happy life filled with love. She was such a wise and peaceful little thing; it always amazed her parents that she seemed to have the wisdom of a very old woman, while at the same time, being an adorable wee girl, innocent and filled with wonder.

Turning off the shower, Robert dried himself quickly and reached for his robe. After running a towel through his hair, he went to the sink and filled it, preparing to shave. He wiped the steam from the mirror, and gazed at the reflection staring back at him from the dampened glass.

Robert thought he looked haggard and drawn. For a man in his early 40s, people had always thought he was much younger than his years. But in recent months, he thought he looked a good deal older. He noticed that he had got a lot more gray hair along his temples, and he was quite salt and peppered throughout his scalp. Though it suited him, he was well aware that it meant there had been a significant toll on his health in recent times.

Taking a good look at his eyes, he noticed that they carried a sadness and a weight that he wondered if anyone else saw when looking at him. Under them, there was a darkness that seemed not to go away any more; it only grew worse with lack of sleep, or slightly better on what he would now call 'a good day', relatively speaking.

Robert wondered if Kathy even saw him any more, or if she ever would again. He missed his daughter, he missed his wife. He missed James, and the unity that there used to be in this family. And he was at a complete loss as to how to fix any of what was wrong.

Many times he wished he could take Kathy's route and just crawl back into bed, pull the duvet over his head and sleep his life away. This was surely one of those days.

The sink was filled, and Robert squirted a mound of shaving gel into one hand; then rubbing both together, he applied the lather to his face. After taking a deep breath, he let out a long sigh as he scraped his face with the razor, and prepared to begin another day.

Elijah had been awake since he heard James come in, so the boy was very tired and pale when he gave up trying to go back to sleep and crawled out of bed. He was nervous about how things might go that day. His Mum was something of a loose cannon, he thought; he and his father were never quite sure what was going to happen with her regarding anything of an emotional nature. Her agreement about James's birthday had caught both the lad and his father off guard. It was entirely unexpected, and both of them thought that something wasn't quite right with regard to Kathy's response. They felt as though they were missing something, and they had been nervous about the birthday ever since.

And finally, the day had arrived. Soon, their questions would be answered. And hopefully, if for no other reason than for James's sake, Kathy could hold it together, just for one day.

But Kathy was not their only concern. James had become so changed, so secretive and so distant in the past few weeks that they had no idea what might be going on in his life, in his heart, or in his mind. No one was even certain that he wanted this celebration, but they were about to find out. Typically, he slept till the early afternoon, so they still had time to prepare. On this particular occasion, neither Kathy nor Robert was aware that he was sleeping in Angelina's room; her door was often closed, and if ever there was a day not to open that door and enter, this was it. Robert and Elijah went to pick up James's birthday gifts as soon as the shops opened. They had already decided on what to buy, but with Robert's work schedule and the short time between deciding to celebrate and the birthday itself, they had not had a chance to collect the gifts. They also did a few other birthday-related errands before heading back to the house in the late morning.

Entering the porch, the house smelled of a baking cake. It had been a very long time since there had been such an event in their home; it gave them hope that Kathy might be returning to her old self, especially when they walked through to the kitchen and there she was, greeting them with a smile and a cheery "Hello!" She seemed very excited, but something did not feel quite right. It was difficult for either Robert or Elijah to put a finger on what was wrong, but there was no mistaking the peculiar atmosphere. They hoped they were just imagining things, and carried their packages upstairs so that James's gifts could be wrapped and his cards made ready.

It was not long before James stumbled out of Angelina's bedroom, and saw his father and brother watching cartoons from Kathy and Robert's bed. Elijah jumped up and ran toward James.

"Happy Birthday, James!" cried the younger of the two boys as he threw his arms around his older brother and squeezed.

This caught James off guard; it had been some time since anyone in the family had attempted to give him a hug, and although his first instinct was to push the lad away, he remembered his love for the boy and allowed the embrace.

"Aren't you excited? It's your birthday!" Elijah fairly squealed with anticipation, hoping that this might be the event that got his family moving forward, and set them on a path of healing. It could be like a birth day for all of them.

“I just woke up, Squirt. Can’t be too excited about anything when I’m not quite conscious yet. Gimme some time to wake up, okay?” He tousled Elijah’s hair as he headed for his own room and a shower.

Elijah’s face fell. He was so hoping that someone was going to be excited about this day besides himself. But so far, no one seemed to feel as positive about it as he did. Sure, Mummy was smiling, but it was not the way his Mum used to look when she was getting ready for a birthday party. Something was wrong.

And although Dad had agreed that James’s birthday should be celebrated, he was awfully quiet and distant. It didn’t feel like he was really there with them. Although that had become the usual state of affairs, Elijah had hoped that maybe for the birthday, Dad would seem to be more involved with the family again.

Elijah climbed back onto his parents’ bed, and curled up with his dad to watch more cartoons. With any luck, this day was going to go well and be a turning point for the family. But given what he knew about them...well, he had good reason to worry that it would go quite another way.

Kathy was downstairs, setting the dining room table for a lovely brunch. It was the first time she had done anything like this since their Christmas celebrations in the weeks before Angelina died, and she was surprised at how good it felt. No one was ever allowed in the kitchen during the decorating of the cake and the lighting of the candles, so traditionally, birthday meals were always held in the dining room.

Kathy even found herself humming as she worked, ironing the lace tablecloth and napkins, reaching into high cabinets for the good dishes; it was going to be a wonderful day.

And when all the food was ready and the table was laid, Kathy called to everyone to meet her in the sitting room. Robert and Elijah brought down the gifts and cards. And James, somewhat surprised that his family had actually prepared a birthday celebration, appeared just moments after he was called.

Kathy and Robert wished James a happy birthday, and gave him hugs and kisses, which made the boy very uncomfortable. Robert also shook his hand and said, "Wow, you're 16. You're a young man now, Son!" and patted him on the back.

Kathy had juice for the boys and coffee for herself and Robert, so everyone had a drink while James opened his gifts. Elijah had bought a beautiful, hard-cover journal, which he said was meant for his brother to use for writing lyrics for his songs. Kathy and Robert had bought a gift certificate for a music store, and also a 'pirate's shirt', as Elijah called it, a gorgeous deep blue, with puffed sleeves, open at the neck but lacing up, 'like pirates wear in films', or so said their youngest boy.

"Try it on, James!! Try it on!" Elijah was bouncing a little on his chair, alive with the first excitement that this family had experienced in months.

One look at James and it was easy to see that he did not particularly want to wear the shirt at that moment; he thought it might make his parents think he had softened his viewpoint of them and the entire family situation. Although they had, indeed, planned a birthday celebration, the young man had not yet forgotten his need to punish his mother and his father for what he saw as their transgressions.

James looked at his parents. It was almost as if he did not recognize them; they were so very changed since Angelina's death. And actually, on thinking about it, since long before her birth. Gone were the warm and happy faces he remembered from years gone by, before all that Dream Baby nonsense began.

'Just look at them now,' he thought, 'so pale and drawn, sad and weak.' And James hated weakness. That's why no one was ever going to see him cry or hurt over Angelina's death. Or anything else, for that matter. The look of contempt that crossed his face was brief, but unmistakable.

Elijah's squeals interrupted James's simmering thoughts. "Come on, James! Please put on your new shirt!"

Deciding that he should not punish his little brother for their parents' failings, he peeled off the shirt he had been wearing, and put on the new one. It was a perfect fit in both style and size, and the colour intensified the beautiful blue in the handsome young man's eyes.

"Oh, James! It's brilliant!" cried Elijah as he leapt out of his chair, clapping his hands together with delight.

This youthful display of enthusiasm came as something of a shock to everyone else present. It felt strange, out of place, uncomfortable. It took only a couple of moments before Elijah noticed the awkward silence in the room. Sadly realizing that no one else shared his excitement, his face fell, and he sank back into his chair, his heart sinking right along with the rest of him.

Elijah glanced from one face to the next. His mother was staring blankly at him. His father looked completely and utterly defeated, drained and lifeless. And James...well, Elijah could not identify the expression at all. The older boy was looking at his parents with a sort of sneer, his eyes flashing ever so slightly. Was it anger? Was it scorn? Was it betrayal? Elijah did not know. But he was certain that it was a sign of worse things to come.

Breaking the uneasy silence, Elijah tried once again to invite some enthusiasm to the little party. "Go on, James. Open the big one." But it was obvious that his own excitement had waned; his discouragement was quite evident.

Elijah pushed a very large, beautifully wrapped box toward James. Inside was a guitar that he had been eyeing for a very long time. In fact, he had been wanting it since before Angelina died, and he was astonished that anyone remembered it.

As angry as he was with his parents, James managed to thank them for this wonderful gift, but his stilted words were delivered with an icy tone. All the best gifts in the world could not make up for what they had done to him, for the pain that Angelina's existence had caused in this family, both long before her death, and in the time since.

James took his gifts to his room. It was a good excuse to spend some time alone. As much as he was furious with his parents, some part of him knew that they had tried to do something good that day, and he could not bring himself to be as unkind as he might have liked.

Sitting on his bed with his new guitar, he was rather confused about the whole day; in part, he was very happy to see that his family had not forgotten or ignored his birthday. But his Mum seemed really strange, and with everyone being so distant, it all felt quite phony and this bothered the young man.

James sat in contemplation, mindlessly plucking at the strings on his guitar. He had to acknowledge that although his parents had made an enormous mess of the family, they had made an effort to fix things by celebrating his birthday. Maybe he could cut them a little slack, at least for the day. Maybe he could try to make the best of it. They had obviously gone to a lot of trouble, especially his Mum. He had not seen her do anything like this kind of cooking or meal preparation since before Angelina died. He was afraid to hope that it meant she might be okay sometime soon. Better to just expect the worst. At least, that way, there were no disappointments. But this? All this 'normal' activity in one day? He had not expected this at all. And it really confused the very sensitive young man.

Sighing, James turned his attention to his guitar. It was too much work to think or to feel anything about his family any more.

It was not long before Robert was knocking on James's door, telling him that lunch was ready.

James got up from his bed, and put the guitar away. The flood of confusing emotions washing through him, he took a deep breath before putting his hand on the doorknob and turning it, preparing to face his family once again and try to give them a chance to put things right.

As James entered the dining room, he found his father and his brother staring at the table, motionless, speechless. The table had been laid for five, just as it would have been if Angelina had been there, with smaller dishes, cutlery and Angelina's special Eeyore cup (Eeyore being her favourite character in the Winnie-the-Pooh books) in the place at the table where she used to sit. And there was Kathy, fussing with an arrangement of flowers, humming while she worked. Yes, humming. And behaving as if nothing in the world could possibly be wrong. Or at least, nothing in *her* world.

She did not seem to notice the disconcerted expressions on the three faces staring at her. And it was impossible for her to imagine what her family was thinking. She could not begin to know the fear that they felt, wondering whether or not she had finally walked through the door to insanity.

But she was ready for them to be puzzled, and that was all she chose to see. As each of them stood staring at the fifth place setting, she spoke. "I hardly think there should be a problem with us acknowledging that today would have been Angelina's fifth birthday. After all, is any one of us not thinking about it today?"

Well, she had them there. Of course, they were all thinking of their Little Angel. And maybe Kathy was right. Maybe this was a good thing. Maybe it was time they started talking about Angelina now and then.

Kathy served their brunch, and would not even let Elijah help. It was a simple but beautiful meal, and everyone enjoyed the food very much. The atmosphere, however, was another story. There was such a strange undercurrent, it was really disturbing. It seemed to be stemming from Kathy, yet no one could identify just what was going on.

After the brunch dishes were cleared away and it was time for the cake, Kathy disappeared for a few minutes into the kitchen. She returned with small serving plates and forks, and a fresh pot of coffee. Back to the kitchen she went, and in another moment, she was back with a beautifully decorated cake, which was covered with candles.

It looked like there must be more than sixteen, but with everyone singing 'Happy Birthday' to James, as Kathy stood, holding the pretty cake beside him, no one was counting them.

Just as the singing ended, she leaned over and placed the cake squarely above the space between James and Angelina's place settings. Kathy was beaming, so proud of herself for having baked and decorated a birthday cake, given her mental and emotional state during the previous few months. But in seconds, the faces of everyone else present fell as they saw "Happy Birthday, James and Angelina" written on the cake, and they counted twenty-one candles. Sixteen for James, and five for Angelina.

The silence was deafening. And Kathy was the only one who did not notice. She told James to make a wish and blow out the candles, which he did, too stunned to do anything else, while his mother chatted away while cutting the cake and putting it on serving plates. She passed them around the table, one at a time, acting as if nothing was wrong. First, she cut a large piece for James and set it down in front of him. There was a piece for Robert, one for Elijah, and another for herself.

Everyone present was holding his breath, waiting to see what Kathy was going to do next, hoping and praying that it wouldn't be what they feared. All eyes were on her, and no one dared move.

And then it happened. Just after Kathy placed James's piece of cake in front of him, she did it. She raised the knife above the cake again, and cut a much smaller piece, and put it on Angelina's plate.

You could have heard a pin drop. The room went absolutely dead silent. Finally, Kathy was going to have to make some excuse for her behaviour. She was certainly right about her family not understanding, but her plan had at least helped her to cope with James's birthday. She had been having a delightful day, imagining that Angelina was there, helping to bake and decorate the cake, imagining that her Little Angel was sitting in the chair at the table, participating in the family's celebration.

But she had a story ready for everyone, and the time had come to share it with them.

"I don't know why you all find it so odd that I just wanted to acknowledge little Angelina one last time. We will never again have a birthday celebration for her, and I just wanted to honour her memory in this way. Besides, I believe she is really here with us anyway; I want her to know we will never forget her."

Everyone was quiet. Though Kathy's words made sense, somehow they just did not seem to be entirely sincere. Her voice was strained and her face too tight. And they did not know just exactly how truthful she was being when she said she believed Angelina was right there with them...if only they knew what she really meant.

James was the first to react. Without a word, he stood, shoving his chair back and knocking it to the floor as he hurriedly pushed past his mother and ran to his room, taking the stairs a few at a time. They heard the door slam and once again, there was a deafening silence.

"Elijah, let's help your mother clean up from lunch," Robert suggested quietly, frightened more than ever about his wife's mental state, and very concerned about how this incident had affected Elijah. And as the boy stood to obey, Kathy told him not to bother, saying that she could manage everything just fine on her own. Her voice now chilly, and her manner rather taut, Robert thought it best that he leave her to it. Thanking her for her efforts and telling her it was a lovely meal, he left the room, his hand on Elijah's back, steering him up the stairs ahead of him.

Elijah went to his room, needing to be alone for a while. Robert followed him, wanting to speak with him but not having any idea what to say.

"Eli, maybe we should talk about this," he began.

Elijah wanted to forget the entire matter. The birthday celebration had been a disaster, start to finish, and it had only served to emphasize all that was wrong with this family. There was nothing that his dad could say to help him now, and he really just wanted to be left alone. Besides, the boy was certain that his father was struggling to deal with his own feelings about all of it, and Elijah decided that the last thing his dad needed was to worry about anyone else's on top of everything else.

"No, Dad, really. I'd rather not. Let's just forget it," he said, his tone leaning towards pleading.

Robert was torn. He knew as a father that he should try to encourage a conversation at that moment, but he was at a loss about where to begin or what to say. Gratefully, he allowed Elijah to let him off the hook, telling the boy to let him know if he changed his mind. Overwhelmed, Robert closed Elijah's door and made a hasty retreat to the bedroom. Putting on a sweater, he grabbed his trainers, having decided to go for a walk.

James was gathering up a few joints and some cash, having been on the phone with Billy who was about to come and pick him up. He wasn't hanging around this nut house one more moment. It was his birthday and he was going to go out and celebrate, no matter what anyone here thought about it.

He'd had enough of being with dead people. The spectre of Angelina's memory haunted him day and night, but James had learned that you don't have to be in the frozen ground to be dead. His parents were certainly proving *that* point and he was sick of death. It hung in that house like the stench of decaying flesh, heavy, pungent, overwhelming and suffocating. It was everywhere, screaming at him, tormenting him, forcing its way into his brain, tearing into his soul, violating every part of his life and his being.

As he was getting ready to leave, he saw his dad walking across the yard, heading toward the woods in the general direction of the place where James and Angelina used to spend so much time together. The lad had not been there since his sister died, nor could he imagine ever going there again. He watched his father until it was hard to see him amongst the trees, and as he stared after his dad, he fed his fury, ensuring that the raging fire within him only grew.

Billy drove up, breaking into James's thoughts. And as he ran down the stairs to meet his friend, James could only think of how relieved he was to be leaving this crazy house of death.

Ten

Angelina had been lying next to James while he slept on her bed during the early morning hours of their birthday. She was petting Frank and rubbing her brother's back now and then, and mostly was just enjoying their time together.

As always, she was practicing all she had learned to try to communicate with her family, but she did not think she was very successful. That was okay. She knew they needed to get used to being without her, and she could still be with them, so it was all fine with her.

Elijah certainly had not had much sleep that night; he was worrying so much about everyone. Angelina really wished that he could just step back and let everyone learn their lessons in their own time. And of course, she also saw that he was still a kid who needed his family. He was so much more quiet and lonely than he had ever been before, and that was saying something.

It had been nice to see Mummy and Daddy curled up together for a while that morning, even though Daddy didn't really know about it. It had been a long time since they had acted like married people. They rarely spoke, and when they did, it wasn't about anything very important. They no longer spent any time together, except when they were sleeping. But even that was different; they used to be curled up together a lot, just like they were that morning, only before, they both liked it that way. And that, along with everything else in the family, had changed a lot. The Little Angel could not help but wonder if or when everything would change back so her family could be happy again.

To make matters worse, Mummy had done that scary thing again. She was talking to her Little Angel the entire morning while she got everything ready for James's birthday party. She was playing 'Let's Pretend' again. She was not speaking as though she realized where Angelina really was; she was asking for her help with baking the cake, and preparing the food.

It upset Angelina to see that her Mummy was playing this game again, and this time was even scarier than the last time, although she wasn't sure she understood why.

No wonder it all fell apart when they saw the cake. Mummy tried to make them think she was doing something right, but she really wasn't, so of course they knew it. She should not have put Angelina's name on the cake, and she *really* should not have cut a piece for a daughter who was dead! Her excuses did not make much sense to anyone, and if Mummy did not stop playing 'Let's Pretend' soon, something bad was going to happen.

Elijah needed to have a really good talk with Angelina after the birthday disaster, so she joined him in his room and let him pour his heart out to her for a long time. At first, the words fell out in a rush for quite a while. And finally, they came a little slower and a little slower still, and eventually, he had no more words to say. But he had many tears to express the rest of the hurt and fear. Angelina went and stroked his hair at that point, and she thought he might have felt it because he seemed a bit startled, looking up and around the room at just that moment.

Communicating was bound to be easiest with him, so it was easy to practice her new skills with Elijah. but the others in the family sure needed it way more than he did. Angelina thought that if only Mummy, Daddy and James knew she was still with them, it would diminish their pain and everyone could begin to heal. They were all in such a mess, but especially James and Mummy. The Little Angel was determined to learn to communicate with them, but she knew that it would take time. Unfortunately, the way things were going, they did not seem to have a lot of that to spare.

Staring out the window, watching his father disappear into the woods, James had bounded down the stairs upon seeing Billy's car coming up the drive. He opened the front door of the cottage at about the same time that Billy was reaching for the bell. "Hey. Thanks for coming to get me, Billy," he said, more grateful than his friend could ever imagine.

"No problem, man. Hey, happy birthday."

"Really rather you didn't mention it again," snarled James.

"Whoa! What happened?"

James's head snapped round to face Billy, and the glower spoke for him. Billy held his hands up in front of his face, palms toward his friend, as he said, "Never mind, mate. Forget it. Sorry."

The two got into Billy's car, and with music blasting, Billy backed up, turned the car around, and headed down the road.

"Where to, man?" he asked his friend.

"Don't care," replied James as he took a joint out of his pocket and dug for some matches. "Anywhere but here." And finding one match left in the pack of them that he got from Mad Dog's, he was happy to know he would soon be feeling very much better.

They rode in silence for some time, James often keeping his eyes closed, leaning his head back against the seat. Just about the time that Billy was pulling up at Mad Dog's, James opened his eyes, and on realizing where they were, he broke into a sly grin.

Billy was a bit disconcerted by James's demeanor. There was something different going on inside his friend on that day, and it had Billy wondering what was up. But James had made it clear he did not wish to discuss it; therefore, Billy respectfully said nothing. Having arrived at the seedy little pub, the two rapped at the back door, which was propped open a little on this pretty spring day, and walked in, calling a greeting to Mad Dog as they passed him in the kitchen. Mad Dog was in the middle of making a sandwich for a customer, a cigarette dangling from his lips as he piled several thin slices of meat on top of a thick piece of bread. Turning to nod at the boys, acknowledging them with a half-smile and a wink, a length of ash fell from the cigarette and landed on the pile of meat.

Mad Dog didn't skip a beat. Using a knife to flick the ash off the meat, he then plunged it into a jar of mayonnaise, pulling out a large dollop of the dressing and spreading it on the second slice of bread. James had done such a good job of shutting off his feelings, he noticed that he had watched this little incident without caring even a tiny bit for the poor sap who was going to eat that sandwich. Somewhere inside himself, he realized that he must be in serious trouble to be so completely lacking in emotion at the moment, not that he cared about the customer or the sandwich; that wasn't such a big deal. It was the fact that suddenly, he seemed to have switched something off entirely. But it was such a blessed relief after the fire storm that had been raging inside him for so long, most certainly he did not care.

Being the middle of the afternoon, there was not much business in the pub, but there was a group of bikers who had been there on other occasions. Most of them seemed to be okay, never giving anyone any grief. But a few of them were pretty rough, and appeared to be on the dangerous side.

And in James's mood on his birthday, that suited him just fine. After what happened at home, he was looking for trouble. He sauntered across the pub and sat down at a table with two of them. Billy was a little bit nervous; he had not anticipated that James would be so bold, at least not with *those* guys! But of course, he wasn't about to let anyone see him feeling like a chicken.

It would have been one thing to deliberately sit at a table beside these large, frightening-looking men. It was entirely another thing for James to stroll on over and join them, uninvited, and strike up a conversation with them. Trying to look as brave as James was obviously feeling, Billy joined them, too, a bit on the hesitant side, but it didn't take him long to slide into his smooth-talking charming ways. That kid could sell refrigerators to Eskimos when he got going.

James quickly became quite chummy with the largest of the bikers. They called him Bull because of his size, and James was betting that he had an unpredictable temper to suit his nickname as well. He was a hairy, scruffy man, with the meanest look in his eyes that James had ever seen on a human being. He felt as though his own looked that way, although no one had ever said anything about it if they did.

Bull had a load of tattoos, and all the ones that were visible were pictures of something violent. They had to do with swords through hearts, or axes cutting off heads, blood everywhere... James was a bit surprised that someone would actually tattoo such things on his body. And he was also intrigued by the notion.

Before long, James and Bull were having quite a lively conversation. Billy joined in, wanting to be on the inside of this group because he was probably much safer that way, now that his friend had got the two of them involved with these guys.

They sat for a long time with Bull and his pals. There was one particularly wild-looking man they simply called Crazy, who was seated on the other side of Bull. Mostly, James and Billy just spoke with these two, as the others were at the tables behind their new buddies.

As the day wore on and the drinks kept flowing, the two boys got to thinking that these guys were going to be their best friends for life. They could not believe that they had ever been afraid of such men, and what was even better was that they felt untouchable, protected, safe, knowing that these guys were on their side.

Eventually, Billy excused himself to go and speak with Mad Dog about one of their 'business deals'. And while he was gone, Bull took the opportunity to lean in and have a private word with

James, asking whether he was interested in having a *real* party. He was giving James a knowing look, as he lowered his head and said, “I don’t know if your friend is into this but I think you are. We know your buddy sells a lot of drugs for Mad Dog, but he doesn’t strike me as the type to try anything really good. Am I right?”

James was somewhat startled. If he had to think about it, Bull was probably right. Billy was good at talk, but not necessarily as brave as he seemed, so there might not be much substance to his words.

“Whatcha got in mind, mister?” asked the boy.

A sly grin crossed Bull’s face and his eyes lit up. Raising one eyebrow, he checked to see that Billy was still busy with Mad Dog behind the bar. Turning to James, he asked, “Ya wanna blow blue?”

The lad had no idea what Bull meant; his puzzled expression did not go unnoticed by the large man. Lowering his voice and leaning in a little closer to James, he replied, “Coke, man. Wanna blow a little?”

Surprised to find himself sitting in a seedy pub with a biker named Bull who was offering him cocaine, James suddenly found the whole thing rather entertaining and he tried desperately to stifle a laugh. But it was too much to keep inside and he cracked up. This was not the response Bull was expecting, and he sat back in his chair, mildly annoyed, not sure what to make of this boy.

James looked at Bull apologetically and said, "I'm sorry, man, but I just had the weirdest day till I got here, and that was just the perfect topper. Yeah, sure, why not? Thanks, I'll give it a try. But I don't have much cash on me."

"No sweat. My party today. What about your little friend?" asked Bull.

"Billy? He's cool, don't worry about him. I've known him all my life; I trust him. Besides, he runs for Mad Dog, he's safe."

"Follow me," said Bull, getting up from the table. The two headed into the men's room. Bull herded James into a stall, and closed the door so the two of them were inside. Bull dumped a bit of white powder on the top of the metal toilet paper dispenser, and using the cover of a book of matches, scraped it into a long line. Digging into his pocket, he pulled out a ten pound note, and rolling it into a tight little tube, he used it to inhale the cocaine into one nostril, while holding the other one shut with a thick finger.

James was tingling with excitement and nervousness. He had not felt so alive in months. He loved the sense of adventure that came with this newest experience, and the rebellion factor was over the top. It was perfect!

Bull dumped a little more of the powder onto the toilet paper dispenser, and James needed no assistance for the rest. He snorted his first hit of cocaine like a pro. Bull slammed him on the back in a congratulatory fashion, while letting out a loud belly laugh.

The two returned to their table, just as Billy was finishing up with Mad Dog. The three sat at about the same time, and Billy could see that something was different in James, who was smiling and exuberant, not at all the way he had been for months. Even when he drank or smoked pot, James didn't get like this. Billy knew right away that James had just tried something new.

At that point, James didn't much care who knew what he had done. He felt great! It was exhilarating! He felt so alive and alert, like he was on top of the world! He could feel his heart racing in his chest, and he seemed to have boundless energy. He knew what it would be like to be Superman! He felt like he could do anything!

Billy was watching and listening while James was flying on coke, and could see when shortly thereafter, it started to wear off for both his friend and Bull. And back to the men's room they went, while Billy waited at the table, not really sure what to make of this. In part, it looked like James was having such a great time, he wondered if he should try it, too. But he was also a little afraid of coke; he knew it was one of the more dangerous drugs and although he was a bit wild, he wasn't stupid. He decided to sit back and say nothing for now, and to do nothing as well.

In a few minutes, Bull and James returned, flying again. By this time, it was early evening, and Billy was getting hungry. Taking a look at the menu, he decided on a cheeseburger and chips.

"I'm starving, James. Let's get some food. Take a look at this. What do you want?" he asked his friend.

James shoved the menu back across the table toward Billy. “Nah, I’m not hungry. Just want a little more whisky! And I’m thirsty. I could use a soda, too.”

“Okay, whatever you say,” replied Billy, and off he went to place his order with Mad Dog, leaving James to Bull and their coke.

In the hours since James had stormed out of the dining room, Robert had been struggling to make sense of Kathy’s behaviour that morning. He had spent a long time walking in the woods where he could be completely alone in the silence of the outdoors. He was so glad they lived in the country, especially at times like this when he needed peace and solitude.

He had walked for some time, following the creek as it wound its way through the trees. It was such a lovely spring day, very sunny and warm, not a cloud in the sky. It almost felt like the Universe was mocking him; his life was about as imperfect and messed up as this day was perfect and beautiful.

For a while, he had been feeling as though Kathy should see someone, a psychologist perhaps. And he was quite certain that if he suggested it, she would flatly refuse. It was four months since Angelina died, and if anything, Kathy seemed to be getting worse instead of better.

Robert sat down on a large, flat rock right beside the creek, and stared into the shallow water. He was certain that Kathy was using more than just the tranquilizers he had prescribed, but every time he even hinted at the idea, she became enraged. He had tried to stop writing prescriptions for her, but that had made her equally angry. He felt trapped; like a hostage. It seemed there was no way out of this nightmare. The house was so oppressive, as though a thick, dark cloud hung inside. Many times, he found himself checking to see that the shades were up and the curtains open; it felt so dark that it had become a physical, tangible thing. It was as though all the life and energy had been sucked out of the house and its inhabitants on the day that Angelina died.

Except, of course, for Elijah, who managed to keep his head above water for some reason, though Robert did not really understand how. It was a puzzle; how does a ten-year-old boy keep his head and spirit sorted when his four-year-old sister dies? And how does he also manage to take on most of the running of the house as well?

Robert was, indeed, grateful for Elijah and his assistance, but of course, this also added to his guilt. He did not think he could possibly feel more inadequate than he already did, but he had said that to himself before, and he did, in fact, manage to feel even worse in time.

After sitting and staring into the water for some time, he was no further ahead in finding any answers to the questions about how to fix all that was wrong in his family. Finally, he rose and began the journey back to the house. And when he got there, he was going to seek out Elijah and see if the boy wanted to do something with his dad.

Arriving back at home after being away a few hours, he searched the house for Elijah and was surprised to find that the boy was nowhere in sight. As expected, James was gone, and he assumed Kathy was asleep or in bed as usual, since the bedroom door was closed.

'Well,' he thought, 'I might as well go to the hospital for a while. There's plenty to do in my office. At least there, I'm useful.' Quietly opening the door so as not to disturb Kathy any more than was necessary, he entered the darkened room. Stepping inside his wardrobe, he pulled the door behind him and snapped on the light. Choosing some clean clothes, he turned out the light and left the bedroom to change in the children's bathroom, hoping not to bother his wife.

Within minutes, Robert was out the door and in his car, having left a note for his family, advising them of his plans.

The drive to the hospital was always enjoyable for Robert, unless of course he was heading in for an emergency. He had always liked driving, and especially in such beautiful surroundings. It restored and refreshed his spirit on the way to and from work each day, and Heaven knew he could sure use that.

Pulling into his reserved stall in the car park, it was obvious to him that it was a Saturday. Although the lot was full of visitors' vehicles, most of the doctors' stalls were empty. It was a good day to get some paperwork done. Though he had previously rebelled about working on weekends because of his family, now it seemed that they had become the reason for him to want to be here on this Saturday, and quite possibly many more. That thought made him feel just awful, but it was the glaring truth.

Robert stopped at the cafeteria for a cup of coffee and realizing that it had been many hours since the birthday brunch, he put a sandwich on the tray as well, although he was not particularly hungry. Walking through the quiet corridors, he was relieved when he made it to his office without passing anyone he knew. The last thing he needed was conversation after such a disastrous day.

Arriving at his office, he dug in his pocket for his keys and with one hand holding the tray, he unlocked the door and snapped on the light. He took a deep breath and let out a long sigh as he leaned against the door while closing it, the overwhelming weight from the day diminishing in the privacy of this room.

Setting the tray on his desk, Robert sat in his big swivel chair, elbows resting on his thighs, and his hands clutching the sides of his head. It was such a relief to be out of the house, such a relief to be alone where it was quiet and he did not have to feel that horribly oppressive dark cloud.

After sitting for a few moments and not moving, Robert ran his fingers through his hair. Then rubbing his face with one long, slow, swipe of his hands, he shook his head, and reached for his coffee. Eyeing the sandwich, he had absolutely no interest in touching it, and thought he might eat later. Picking up the first paper in his inbox, he began to work.

Elijah had come home not long after his father left for the hospital. He had merely gone for a bike ride, tired of being stuck in the house which was such an unhappy place to be. He had enjoyed a long chat with Angelina, or at least, he believed he had, and with James and Dad gone, and his Mum in bed again, he thought his bike would be a great means of escaping what had come to feel like insanity in their house.

The boy was disappointed when his father had gone to work, and he contemplated phoning to see if he would come back. Deciding against it, he thought maybe his dad just needed to escape the insanity, too.

And little did anyone know, James had just stepped into a whole new kind of insanity on that very day.

Eleven

By the middle of the evening, James and Bull had each done several lines of coke, and Billy was starting to worry about his friend. He had never seen anyone dive into it so fast and so hard, and knew that with James's general emotional state for the past while, this was bad news. But he knew better than to try to stop his friend; James was so volatile; he was likely to explode if he was going to react at all. So he decided to keep his mouth shut and just see what happened.

So far, James seemed to be handling it okay. He wasn't having any negative effects that were obvious, he just seemed to be having a great time.

Later in the evening, Bull said it was time to get going. He and Crazy rose from their seats and said goodbye to James, who thanked his new friend profusely for the great time.

"Sure, James. Glad you had a blast. See you again soon, right, Buddy?"

"You bet, Bull."

And with that, the two large men exited the pub, and in moments, the customers inside heard their bikes roaring off into the night.

James and Billy were quiet for a few moments. James was contemplating the wonders of cocaine, and Billy was trying to decide what to make of the entire situation. He got a couple of sodas for them, and another order of chips since it had been a few hours since he had eaten his burger. James picked at the chips a little; he had not had any food since brunch, and with cocaine destroying his appetite, he was just now beginning to be a bit hungry as he was coming off the drug.

He also noticed that he felt extremely exhausted and thought he might crash and just fall asleep, sitting right there in the bar. He drank the soda that Billy had brought to him, and after they finished their drinks and the chips, they left the pub, calling "G'night, mate!" to Mad Dog.

It was not long before James fell asleep while Billy drove, and he slept almost all the way home. Upon arriving in front of the house, James thanked Billy for a great birthday, and got out of the car.

It was after midnight; the house was dark, except for the few lights that his dad always left on for him when he was out. James headed straight for bed, elated about his new experience and his exciting day. And he was pumped about the next time he would get to do a little coke.

Robert heard James arrive, but he was already settled into bed and knowing James's unwillingness to communicate, figured there was no point in getting up to say hello or anything else. Better to leave James for tonight, and maybe tomorrow, they could talk about what happened earlier with the birthday cake.

It had been such a bizarre day, beginning with Kathy's strained cheerfulness and her unbelievable words about the reason for the cake having Angelina's name on it, and for there being a place setting for her, as well as having a piece of cake put on her plate.

He hated feeling relieved about having been at the hospital for several hours on a Saturday, but had anyone else described the same situation to him, he was certain he would have supported those feelings entirely.

It had been good for him to go to the office that afternoon. After he had done a couple of hours' work, he had leaned back in his chair, and stretched his legs out in front of him while clasping his hands behind his head. Lying back like that for a few moments, Robert thought a cold drink was in order.

Picking up his tray with the coffee cup and the sandwich, most of which had been left untouched, he left his office and headed toward the cafeteria once again.

Away from home for a while, Robert felt more cheerful and light, his appetite returning on this early evening. As he stood in the queue, pondering his choices, someone behind him bumped into him, startling him out of his thoughts. Turning reflexively to see who had knocked into him, at the same moment there came a woman's voice.

"Oh, excuse me! I'm so sorry!" The woman behind him spoke with a bit of an accent. "I should be looking where I'm going, not where I've already been!'

Robert smiled. "That's all right. No harm done." Extending a hand, he said, "Robert Lane."

"Rosa Franco." She offered her fingers for a more ladylike 'handshake'. Robert held them lightly and briefly, enchanted by this beautiful Italian woman.

The two made small talk while they made their meal selections. He told her that he was a doctor at this hospital, and she said that she had just begun a job in pharmaceutical sales and would be at the hospital now and then. He was thinking how wonderful that was; he may be able to see her again sometime. And she was thinking it, too.

Since Robert was in front of her in the queue, he was able to purchase her dinner for her before she could argue too much about it. She thanked him, and then said yes when he asked her to join him at a table.

The cafeteria had a large area which was like a greenhouse, filled with many plants and flowers, with lots of windows to allow a good view of the outdoors. It was in this section that the two found a table out of the way, and so began yet another complication in Robert's life. He knew it from the moment he introduced himself. He could have simply turned back after the woman's apology, and not said another word.

But he was well aware that he was ripe for such a situation. He did not want to talk to anyone he already knew personally or at work. That would have been far too messy. At work, he needed to maintain his professional demeanor. And as for speaking with friends, well, it just didn't work for him to discuss what was happening in his family because once this was all behind them, Kathy would be socializing with those people again, and he did not want anyone to be making any negative judgements about her.

When Rosa appeared, it felt as though she had been sent to him. The moment he saw her, something inside him sang, and at the same time, he felt a warning, an ominous 'something'. He was unable to put his finger on it, but he just knew that this meeting was going to change his life, though he could not say how.

The two sat and talked as though they had known each other for years. Robert hardly noticed what he ate; so enchanted was he, so engrossed in the conversation. It did his heart good to sit and talk to someone who did not know anything at all about Angelina or the state of his family since her death. It was simply wonderful, freeing.

Not only did she not know anything about Angelina, he did not have to tell her. It wasn't that he did not love and miss his sweet girl, but his life, every waking minute of it, was being consumed and destroyed in one way or another by the fact that she had died. He wanted a little relief from this, a bit of a reprieve. He wanted just a little taste of normal life again, with laughter and light, instead of nothing but darkness and death.

Robert saw Rosa looking at his wedding band. He felt a bit awkward and he fumbled in his brain for the right words to say, but before he could find them, she looked away and did not mention it. He was greatly relieved; it was another conversation for which he was unprepared, and thankfully, it seemed that it was one he did not have to have.

Rosa was not wearing any rings at all, and although this did not necessarily mean that she was single or unattached, it certainly added to her appeal. Robert's life was already complicated enough, and although meeting this woman could certainly compound the difficulties, he believed that knowing her was also going to make some things a whole lot better.

It was quite a while after both had finished eating that Rosa said, "Well, this has been delightful, Robert. And as much as I'd love to stay and chat for hours, I really must be going."

Robert's heart sank. Of course, it had to end sometime, but he was so caught up in the joy of their time together, he felt like a little kid who was suddenly told he had to leave the playground and go home for a nap. He hesitated, wanting to ask if he could see her again, the words dancing on the tip of his tongue. He felt like a school boy, afraid to ask a girl on a date for the first time.

It was uncanny how this woman seemed to read his mind; there had been several moments throughout the evening when Robert had got this feeling, and here was yet another. Reaching into her pocket, she handed him a card, and told him that he could call her if he wished to do so. Robert was speechless;

this was a dream come true (or was it going to create a nightmare?), and he stumbled over a reply.

Finally, he was able to put a few words together, and told her that he did not have a business card handy, but he could be reached through the hospital, if she felt so inclined. The switchboard would put her through to his direct line, and he would be happy to hear from her sometime.

Pushing their chairs back, they rose and stood facing each other, both noticing yet another awkward moment as it seemed the two were both eager for, yet hesitant about a kiss. Robert managed to compose himself, and warmly taking her hand in both of his, he leaned over and gave her a sweet and gentle kiss on the cheek.

He thanked her for her delightful company, and the two went their separate ways. Robert was blown away by the entire experience. He was filled with all the excitement and anticipation of a school boy, as well as all the guilt of a married man who had no right to feel such things regarding a woman other than his wife.

He tried to tell himself to relax, and he worked hard to justify the situation, insisting that it was never going to be an affair. He told himself that it was just a conversation, that Rosa would just be a friend, and what was the harm in that?

But Robert knew perfectly well that a part of him wanted much more than simple conversation or friendship, and there was an awful lot of harm in *that*.

Struggling to push those thoughts out of his head, he returned to his office to put Rosa's card in a special and hidden place. But locking the door behind him, he knew that trying to get rid of such thoughts was going to be an exercise in futility. The wheels for something huge had been set in motion; already, he had no control over it and he was certain it was going to change his life, though he could not be sure about exactly what that meant. All he could do was wait and see how it played out.

Kathy was soaking in a hot bath when Robert returned. There was not much conversation between them, really just enough to determine that Elijah had ensured that he and his mother had eaten dinner. They had watched a bit of telly together, though Kathy could not tell Robert what they saw or anything about it, since she had not really paid any attention. She was just sitting next to Elijah, unaware that he could feel just how absent and distant she was. To him, it was worse than if she had just not been with him at all.

He was such a patient child, and he believed that someday, his family would be fine again. But sometimes, it seemed like it was just too much for him to bear and he was tired of waiting for everyone to get on with healing. That evening had been one of those times. It was very much unlike him, but at one point, Elijah really struggled not to yell at his mother, "Are you in there???? Hello?? I'm right here beside you, do you know that??!"

He was glad that the show was just ending at that point, and he had a reason to leave the room. The last thing his mother needed was an outburst like that from him. She had enough to deal with; he was the only one in the family who was reasonably well and stable, and if he fell apart, too, well, he shuddered to think what that might do to her and to the others. He was the glue, for now. He was just barely holding this family together. And really, it was ‘just barely.’ But at ten years old, what could they expect?

After Elijah left Kathy and the television, she had gone and sat out on the back porch for a while. The sun was beginning to set; it was nice that the days were getting longer. She sat and stared out at the garden, filling her head with memories of Angelina planting, digging and watering.

And when the sun had gone down, she had headed for her bubble bath, where Robert found her upon his return.

Feeling particularly guilty, Robert was relieved that Kathy was on the other side of their bathroom door when he said hello and chatted with her a little. He felt as though his thoughts of Rosa would be emblazoned on his face. He was happy to change into his dressing gown and leave the bedroom before his wife emerged and could see him.

Stepping into his slippers, he went down to the sitting room, where he picked a book off the shelf, and got comfortable on the settee. It was not long, however, before he realized that he had been reading the same words over and over again. He could not concentrate. All his thoughts were of Rosa, of the light and wonderful feelings he had while he was with her. It was such a blissful 'time out' from his life, and looking back, it was not just his life since Angelina died. It was the four year period during which she was ill and her future was uncertain. It was about every pregnancy which ended in miscarriage. And it was about the guilt and the disappointment that the accident had caused so long ago.

No, it was not just about the difficult time since Angelina died. His life had been dark and troubled for years, yet he had never acknowledged it, choosing instead to put on a strong, happy face and Do The Right Thing. He loved his wife very much; that had never changed. But certainly, through the years, their relationship had changed, though Robert had never questioned it, had never even thought about it. He had always just kept the strong, happy face on, while he Did The Right Thing. And it never mattered what might be missing for him on the inside; his family needed him. He had obligations to them. He was going to do his best to be sure he never let them down.

And for years, he had been plodding along like this, not nearly as happy as others thought him to be for most of the time until Angelina became very ill near the end of her life.

It struck Robert as very odd that a person could live in a state of unhappiness, yet be completely unaware of it. And he did not believe that he had always felt that way; he knew that there had still been some good parts to life with his family. But overall, when he really thought about it, lying there on the settee, he was stunned to realize that for many years, he had not been nearly as content as he had thought.

He had to wonder what this meant for the rest of his family. Had it been the same for all of them throughout that time? Had he been completely blind? He always thought that he and Kathy had been close to their children, and that they had a happy family. But if he was just understanding that his own happiness had been more fantasy than anything, there was a good chance that it was the same for the rest of them during those difficult times since Kathy's accident.

Had it not been for Angelina being a very ill child, and then dying, he believed that her birth would have changed all of that, and they would have been much happier. Well, whatever the reasons, the family was certainly off in its separate corners now, and it only seemed to be getting worse. And today, he had taken several deliberate steps to put himself off in a corner that wasn't even on the map with his family. What was he thinking? What was going to happen?

For these and so many other questions, he had no answers. And he was too tired to even think about them any more. Leaving a few dim lights on for James, Robert climbed the stairs and crawled into bed with his wife, who was asleep - or who was pretending to be. Robert never knew for sure any more. And on this night, for the first time, he did not suppose that he cared.

Twelve

Over the rest of the spring and into the summer, the Little Angel was shocked to see what happened to her family. Her mother had been spending most of each day playing 'Let's Pretend Angelina Is Alive', although after The Birthday Incident, she made certain that Robert and the boys never knew about it. They just did not understand.

So Angelina spent a lot of time with her mother, believing that her communication skills had improved quite a bit, but unable to understand why her mother could not hear her, especially because she knew that she had been successful in varying degrees in the past.

One day, after what she believed was a particularly good attempt at communicating with her Mummy, but

Mummy did not seem to hear her, the Little Angel went to her Teacher.

"I don't understand. A long time ago, there were some moments when I was trying to speak to my Mummy, or when I touched her, and she seemed to know it, at least a little bit. But it seems that for quite a while, the harder I try, the less she is aware! I know I'm getting better at this, because Elijah seems more able to hear me, so I really don't understand! Can you explain it to me? Am I doing something wrong?" asked the puzzled Angelina.

"Oh, no, Dear One, it's not you at all. Your Mummy had been trying to accept your death. At that time, she remembered your funeral, remembered seeing you in your coffin. She understood that you had died. But it got to be too much; she stayed stuck in her room and in her grief for too long, and she could not cope with it.

"In order to protect herself from those feelings, she had to pretend that you are alive. Because she has got further away from believing that you are dead, this is why she cannot sense you now. This is most worrisome; your Mummy is in a very bad way, and something is going to happen that will either push her over the edge or make her accept the realities of her life," replied the Teacher. "She can't go on like this forever, Little Angel. Just keep trying to reach her, and maybe soon she will be ready to receive your messages. We can always hope."

"Now that you've explained it, that makes sense to me, and I'm wondering if it's something like that for Daddy," said Angelina. "He's been spending a lot of time with another lady, and he never, ever talks about me to her. I sit on his lap sometimes, like I used to do, and he doesn't seem to notice me now. Once in a while, I think maybe he wonders if I'm there, but there were times before when I knew he felt me touching him, and I knew that he was sure I was with him.

"But now? Now, it's like I was never there at all. Is that why Daddy can't feel me? Has he forgotten about me? I never thought that would happen!" The Little Angel looked like her heart was breaking.

"No, of course your Daddy has not forgotten you. But life for him has been terribly unhappy for a long time. There are many things troubling him, and with your Mummy being the way she is, and James - well, he's another story, isn't he? - your Daddy just needs to pretend in a way, too. He just needs a little break from being unhappy for so long. But he remembers you very well, Angelina. He thinks about you very many times every day. It was just that he felt like he was suffocating in darkness and sadness, and he needs a kind of 'time out'," explained the Teacher.

"When I used to get a 'time out', it was because I had been a little bit naughty! Has Daddy been naughty? How can a 'time out' be fun?" the confused Little Angel asked.

The Teacher chuckled softly. "It's a different kind of 'time out', Angelina. There's the kind that parents give children so they can think about something they did that was naughty, and hopefully learn not to do it again. And there's the kind that people need sometimes when life gets to be too difficult. It's like recess in school, or a lunch break when people are at work. Everyone needs a break sometimes. Your Daddy will never forget you, I promise. But yes, his 'time out' is why he does not seem to hear you or feel you right now."

The Little Angel was quiet for a few moments, thinking about all the

Teacher had said, the little furrowed brow emphasizing that she was deep in thought. "You said that James is a whole other story. And yes, he is. I am astonished by all that he has been doing in the past few months, Teacher. I am really worried about him. And I'm not reaching him the way I'd like to do either!" The Little Angel was very frustrated.

"Yes, James is really in trouble now, isn't he?" replied the Teacher. "It is so hard to see our loved ones struggling like this. They have lessons they are meant to learn; you know this, Angelina. It was one of the first lessons we taught you on this side. Whatever happens on Earth is meant to be; it happens for a reason, and we must accept it. James needs these experiences, and although they are painful for you to watch, they will ultimately have value for him, whether in this life or another."

"That sounds good, Teacher, but it doesn't really help me to feel better about it," the Little Angel said sadly.

"I know, and you're so young. You will see. Give yourself more time and you will understand everything."

The Little Angel thanked her Teacher and wandered off by herself. It was her usual response after these conversations with the Teacher; she liked to go and think about what she had been told. It helped her to learn, and my goodness, there was so much to learn on The Other Side!

She had been completely shocked when James began his descent into the world of drugs and alcohol. She was especially alarmed by his use of cocaine, which was one of the worst drugs for addiction, health risks and the possibility of death. And because cocaine is very expensive, James had started stealing from people to support his habit. He was getting into all kinds of things and his parents did not even know. They hardly saw him any more. And when they did, he was either elated and manic, or moody and sullen, just wanting to sleep.

Kathy was still so caught up in her own issues that she really did not pay much attention to any of this. Robert was starting to wonder whether James was using drugs, but with James being as volatile as he had been in recent months, Robert really did not believe that he could cope with the fallout of asking the young man such a question. He chose, instead, to believe that his son knew better, especially having grown up with a doctor for a father, and hearing the lectures often enough.

For a while when James first started using cocaine, his friend, Billy, was too scared to try it. But eventually, he saw that James just seemed to have fun with it, and nothing bad happened. Since James kept encouraging him to try, eventually, poor Billy succumbed to the peer pressure, and he wound up getting involved with it as well. Before long, however, neither of them liked the nasty effects that the coke had on their noses, so they resorted to smoking crack, a much more potent form of cocaine.

James soon found that he could not steal enough cash to pay for his crack, so he began dealing. If he went to school at all now, it was to spread the word among the known users of crack and coke there that he was their man. By late spring, the school had contacted Kathy and Robert to let them know that James had refused to attend at all for some time, and when discussions with him yielded no change, eventually, he was expelled.

Not long after James and Billy had got into the cocaine, there was another night when Mike accompanied them to Mad Dog's pub. Home was a pretty unhappy place for him since his parents had split up and were using their children to try to hurt each other. Mike was expected to go to his dad's new apartment on the weekends, and he hated it, especially since his dad now had a girlfriend who was sleeping there. The whole situation gave Mike the creeps and he didn't want any part of being there, or seeing that.

Then it got worse when he would go back home because his mother would grill him about what his dad was doing and with whom. The whole thing was just awful, so bad, in fact, that he thought he should just get in his mother's car and drive off into the sunset, far away from both of his parents. James thought that was a great idea and what had begun as a sort of a joke had now become a potentially serious plan.

But for now, James had a good thing going. He was dealing coke and crack, and was making decent money. It was great not to have to steal any more; that was awkward, clumsy and too dangerous. His parents were too afraid of his temper to give him any grief about where he was or what he was doing, so he had pretty much complete freedom, except he didn't have any wheels. But that would be fixed in time.

It wasn't long before James and Billy let Mike in on their little 'secret', and encouraged him to smoke a little crack. He, like Billy, was scared at first, but they bugged him with 'Aw, just try a little hit, just one, ya big sissy', and other such comments, until he finally relented and figured, well, they seemed to be okay, so he might as well just try a wee bit.

It was fabulous, as far as he was concerned, but it sure hurt his throat. He loved the high; that stuff really killed his depression. Well, until it wore off. The crash was pretty rough. He didn't much like the way he felt when he landed. He was right back in the reality of his depressing life, but it felt even worse because he'd had this incredible high, which made the low feel even lower.

But James and Billy were right there to offer another hit, and off he sailed again. How cool was that?! It didn't take much to find Mike begging for more.

James thought this was just perfect! They had all been good friends for years, and then even when they were going through tough times, they could do that together, too. And to be able to stumble upon this fabulous stuff and to be able to share it with his best pals -- well, James thought this was all just wonderful.

He would have loved to have his own car, and he couldn't wait for that complete freedom. But it was nearly another year until he was 17 and could legally get his driving licence and even think about buying a car. For now, he was just grateful for the use of Billy's car, and he pitched in for petrol and repairs now and then to be fair.

Billy always appreciated that James didn't take advantage of him or his car, and he was glad that James didn't push him to drink more or do more drugs when he was driving. Sure he messed around with those things a bit, but he always backed off for a while before he was getting behind the wheel. The last thing he needed was to get stopped by some cop who was out to bug teenaged boys, and then noticed that he was driving under the influence of some substance or other. He wasn't too worried about accidents; he was very careful. It was just the fact that he had heard lots of stories of cops stopping young guys with some lame excuse, just to be nosy, just to annoy them, or whatever. And he sure didn't want to lose his licence. He felt quite capable of driving while he was stoned, but if he ever got charged for that, oh, man, he couldn't handle the lack of freedom. And he was 18 now, so no more juvenile offences for him; it would all be adult Court. Best to have some fun and try to keep his nose clean. And with a wry smile, and his love of terrible puns, he had to add to himself that that's why he switched from doing coke to smoking crack.

It was amazing to all three lads that Robert had not figured out that James was into crack and cocaine. Well, truth be told, James thought his dad was warming up for a chat about the subject a time or two, but the young man blew him off so fast, he didn't know what hit him. The three friends decided that if Robert was really convinced of it, he would probably try harder to find out the truth, and with that kind of reasoning behind them, they were certain that James's father did not have a clue. Pretty stupid for a doctor, they thought. James just said that his dad was so wrapped up in his own stuff that he couldn't really be bothered to find anything out for sure. He was glad that his dad was leaving him alone. The last thing he wanted was to have his parents find out what was going on; he had a good thing happening and he wasn't too interested in changing any of it.

Billy and James were doing well with their drug runs; Billy was working lots of drugs for Mad Dog, and James had crack and coke covered for Bull. The two boys were quite a team, and they often joked about how cool it would be to write a book about their escapades. They got themselves into some pretty remarkable situations and they saw some really wild stuff.

On this particular evening, they had some drugs to pick up at Mad Dog's, and then they were off to see their customers. Billy had a few deliveries of methamphetamines, some weed and a few other things. James had a few good-sized rocks to go, along with a fair bit of powder. They collected the goods from the pub, and after sticking around for a quick drink, away they went.

The first place was on Billy's usual route. It was the basement of a really rundown little shack at the edge of town, not far from Mad Dog's pub. The boys always preferred to go in together, hoping there might be safety in numbers, though they were well aware that their job was not without significant risks, no matter what they did to stay safe.

In this particular basement, it always smelled of stale urine, and rotting food. It was filthy, beyond description. There were usually at least a couple of young women lying around, often begging for another hit, probably prostitutes, at least they sure looked that way.

There were needles and drug paraphernalia on the floor, on tables. There were always bottles of alcohol sitting around, and the occasional pizza box or other fast food rubbish, but it sure didn't look like anyone actually lived there. However, James supposed everyone had a different view of what that word meant. And to these people, it seemed that to have drugs and alcohol all the time, surrounded by filth and going without proper food was 'living'.

Oh, well, what did he care? They were not his concern. He had a job to do, and he could rationalize the doing of it by telling himself that if he didn't, someone else would. So he might as well reap the benefits, 'cause he sure needed the cash.

There were many places on both their routes that were similar to this one, but there were others which were shockingly opposite. There were beautiful, upscale, expensive homes with people who looked like accountants or lawyers, and they were ready for a party just like the scruffiest hooker who was desperate for her next fix.

James didn't worry about running into anyone he knew on these routes, because if he did, he wouldn't be the only guilty party, and anyone who was needing his services was in just as much of a mess as he was, and would want just as much silence as he did.

Actually, the idea of running into some high-class executive that his parents knew, who was looking for a few rocks of crack, was quite entertaining for him. He would love a chance to stare one of those superior, arrogant, rich pigs in the face, knowing that if they had kids, they'd all be giving them the 'don't do drugs' speeches. They're adults. They're supposed to know better, right? He'd have the excuse of being a misguided kid who has had a difficult time. They would look far worse than he did. The image always made him laugh, sneering at the hypocrisy that existed in most adults.

He thought about what a hypocrite his dad was. There he was, being the great doctor, fixing everybody else's lives and problems, and just look at his own! His life, his family, what a huge mess, and he didn't seem to have a clue that anything was even wrong. Either that or he was too stupid to know what to do. If only his patients knew what a failure he was at home. Funny how he had never seen his dad like this before. He used to really love and respect his dad, but he was different since Angelina died, and James surely did not respect him now.

He knew he would get the big lecture about how he was ruining his life if his parents ever caught wind of his activities, but look at the two of them! His mother was stuffing her face full of pills all the time, his dad didn't seem to notice or care - about that or anything else - so what right would he have to stand there and harp at James about his life and choices?

James had no intention of giving up his new source of income. It was fabulous. Yeah, it was a bit dangerous, but he was smart enough to keep himself safe, and it helped knowing that he and Billy were together, so he wasn't worried about the risks.

And he could have all the crack he wanted. And he wanted quite a lot.

With James having taken up smoking cigarettes some time earlier, he had begun stealing packs of smokes when he could manage it, although now he could afford to buy them. Stealing them had become something of a game because they were behind the counter in shops. But he knew a few places where there were really cute girls working, and he found ways to get behind the counter with them when there weren't other customers close by, and with his arm around the girls, he had got quite good at snatching a few packs and shoving them in his coat pocket. Sometimes, it was a simple con, flirting with them shamelessly and asking them point blank to give him a pack or two, and asking, of course, with his face buried in their necks or in some other way manipulating them with his charms. James was a very handsome young man, and the girls often fell for the bad boy look that he had developed.

Yes, James was, indeed, a whole other story, and his little sister sadly watched from The Other Side as this tale was unfolding. And it did not seem that it could possibly have a happy ending.

Thirteen

Robert and Rosa had been spending a lot more time together as the months had passed since their meeting in the spring. Now, in the late summer, if asked, they would have said they had grown quite fond of one another. And if they were honest, they might have even said they were falling in love.

Their meetings had usually been in remote pubs or restaurants, places where they could just sit and talk, and they spoke about anything other than whatever was going on at home. Robert still did not know whether Rosa was involved with anyone, nor did he want to know. And neither of them ever mentioned the wedding band that Robert wore.

There was no talk of children or family. They spoke only of dreams, of beliefs, of ideals. They told jokes and laughed; they spoke of philosophy. They attended a few art shows. They went to the museum. They spent time walking in parks, holding hands and saying absolutely nothing.

It was as though on their first meeting, there had been an unspoken rule: We do not talk about 'those things', meaning, of course, commitments to partners and children. And it was wonderful that both of them had understood this rule, and had willingly accepted it, with no discussion necessary.

Robert so loved his time with Rosa, but he well knew that it was like a fantasy, that it was not a 'real' relationship. He knew that as soon as either of them introduced the forbidden topics, it would have been ruined. Each of them obviously filled a need in the other for something light, refreshing, and fun. It could not have been more perfect.

It was, however, difficult at times for Robert to remember the fantasy aspect of his relationship with Rosa. There were occasions when he left the beauty of time spent with her, and walked into his dark and oppressive home, only to find his wife curled up in the bedroom, blinds down on a lovely summer day, and his heart sank. He had to admit that it was becoming increasingly difficult to leave Rosa in a 'fantasy' place in his heart and in his mind. And the longer Kathy was a mess, the harder it became to want to repair his marriage.

Kathy's doctor had cut back her sleeping pills over the past few months, but he was still allowing her something when she felt she needed it. Unfortunately, that was pretty much every night, but since her prescriptions would run out before he would refill them, she had taken to having a few shots of whisky or some wine to help her to sleep. And sometimes, she used them to get through the day.

Because she spent some time tossing and turning at night, and was often lying awake while Robert slept, she had occasion to hear Robert mumbling when he had bad dreams. Usually, she would gently shake him when that happened, rousing him only enough to stop the dream and calm him. She wondered whether she moaned and thrashed around like he did; after all, she was still having horrific nightmares on a regular basis. They never seemed to leave her. It felt like she could not win; if she was awake, she had to face the reality that Angelina was dead. And if she was asleep, well, it was there as well, but usually with terrifying or violent things happening around it.

Kathy was finding that pretending Angelina was still alive was really helpful to her. It made it so much easier for her to get through the day, and still she could not understand why Robert and the boys had got so upset about it all those months ago. She was not yet particularly functional, but at least she was managing on fewer tranquilizers and sleeping pills than she'd had to take initially, and between her fantasies about Angelina being alive, and the odd top-up of alcohol here and there, she was managing to get a little gardening done, and she was, in fact, preparing more meals and had begun resuming her duties.

She was well aware that she had a long way to go, but for heaven's sake, they couldn't expect her to just snap back to the way she had been before Christmas Day, could they?

She believed that everyone needed different crutches and assistance to get them through tough times, and she decided that no one had the right to tell her that her way was wrong. She was certain that her comforting thoughts were not nearly as dangerous as her dependence on pills and alcohol. And she was very wrong.

One night, she was lying in bed, unable to sleep. Robert began to moan and move around as if he was having a nightmare again. His head was thrashing back and forth on the pillow and he began to say, "No! No!"

Kathy watched him for a moment, and then began to reach across to stroke his head and try to settle him. But before she could touch him, he said, "No, Rosa! Don't go!"

Kathy's hand froze in mid-air, suspended above Robert's forehead. She was stunned. Who was Rosa? Was this someone he knew? Was this a patient? She tried to think of all possible places he could have met someone named Rosa, so as not to jump to conclusions, but with the state of their marriage, she had trouble believing that there was anything innocent about this woman's involvement in her husband's life.

Kathy pulled away from Robert, and turning her back to him, she crept as close as she could get to the edge of the bed, almost hanging over it in an effort to put as much distance as possible between her husband and herself. Her heart was pounding and her stomach rolled as a new fear raced through her soul. She thought about the past several months, searching for clues as to whether or not Robert was seeing someone else.

Her first feeling was anger, immediately followed by betrayal, thinking that her husband could take up with someone else under circumstances such as these. Their precious daughter had died; should they not have stuck together through that time? How could he turn to someone else?

And there it was. Like a bag of bricks hitting her right between the eyes, there it was. How well she knew the answer to that question. The reality of who she had been, or at least what kind of wife she had been for months, *that* was how he could do it. How many times had Robert come to her offering or needing comfort? And on every single one of those occasions, she had pushed him away or at the very least, ignored him. She had never consoled or comforted him throughout the time since Angelina died, nor had she allowed him to comfort her. For Pete's sake, she had not even allowed him to touch her! She had hidden away in their room most of the time, she was a ghost of a woman, who had built a very thick wall around herself, and she was stunned to realize that she had not seen it until now. At least, not like this. Not even close.

Oh, what were the signs? She knew she had heard all the signs that might mean a spouse was having an affair. What were they?? Her brain was so thick from months of drugs, alcohol and depression, it was as though her thoughts were all stuck in quicksand, struggling to surface. Let's see, there was something about showering more often or using colognes more frequently. Did those fit? Think! Come on, you must be able to notice if there's a difference there!

As hard as she tried, she really had nothing to draw on. She had paid so little attention to Robert in recent months, she had no idea what he wore from one day to the next, when or whether he showered, or whether he had been wearing cologne or not.

She was certainly going to have to start paying attention and see whether there was reason to ask him who Rosa was.

It was a very long time until she finally drifted off into a restless sleep. Thoughts were spinning and swirling in her head, and she could not settle, imagining Robert with another woman. Overcome with guilt, she was sick with the realization that she had driven him there. She might as well have found the woman for him herself, introduced them and planned their first date. And every other.

It was going to be a very long night. If ever there was a night she wanted a sleeping pill, this was it. But something told her that it would be a big mistake. After all, isn't that a huge part of how she got here?

No, she was not going to escape into a haze of drugs again. Not if there was any way she could help it.

The next day, Kathy made a concerted effort to be awake when Robert was getting ready to go to work. Not having had a pill to help her sleep made a difference. For once, she was not in a drugged fog when his alarm went off.

She was extremely tired, and looked like she had been through at least one war, but she managed to get herself out of bed while he was in the shower. She even got as far as the kitchen, and made a pot of coffee, which was just finished brewing by the time her husband entered the kitchen.

"Good morning, Robert. I thought you might like some coffee before you went to work."

His eyes grew wide with surprise. "I thought I smelled coffee! It's so early! I didn't think it would be Elijah, but I certainly didn't expect it was you! What a treat! Thank you!"

And with that, Robert took half a step toward his wife, wanting to give her a hug and a kiss, but with months of training, he stopped abruptly. Fixing his tie in an effort to erase his blunder, he shifted uncomfortably from one foot to the other, not quite knowing what he should say next.

Kathy could not help but notice that Robert had almost gone to her in an affectionate manner but stopped himself. It stung, but she had to admit her responsibility in creating this situation. She was light years away from being able to discuss it just then, but she was making the best effort that she could to change it.

She poured two cups of coffee, and handed one to Robert before sitting down at the table. Both of them were well aware of how awkward this moment was. They had been married for so many years, shared a house, a bed, their lives, three children, yet they felt like complete strangers, and neither knew what to do next. Neither knew what to say. Robert pulled up a chair and sat for a few moments, sipping his coffee, frequently looking at his watch, but not even paying attention to the time; it was just something to relieve the awkwardness of doing nothing.

Eventually, he rose from his chair and said, "Well, I'd better get moving. I, uh, hope you have a good day, and thanks for making the coffee. That was nice."

Another awkward moment, knowing this was where the husband was supposed to kiss the wife goodbye, but she sat on one side of the table and he stood on the other. Finally, with each of them wondering what to do next, Robert cleared his throat, turned to the door and left without another word.

Kathy sat for a while, unsure of what to make of their moments together that morning. Clearly, he was uncomfortable around her, but it wasn't much better for her being with him either. How on earth did there get to be such a huge gap between them? Where had all the time gone? How could she have pushed him away for so long? She had always leaned on him before; what was it that caused her to shut him out?

She had many things to work out, many issues to consider. Her life, her marriage, everything was in a huge mess, and she had no idea where to begin trying to put it all right again. Her first inclination was to go and take a tranquilizer. She rationalized that it was a particular difficult day, given what had just happened, but then, something inside her struggled to bubble up through her denial, and she knew that maybe she shouldn't that day, at least not just then. Kathy realized that she needed to try to keep a clear head, although she was not certain that she could get through the whole day without a pill.

She did know, however, that she was willing to try.

Robert made his way along the winding country lanes on his way to the hospital, his mind drifting back to the events of the morning. He had been rather bewildered when he emerged from the bathroom after his shower, certain that he smelled coffee brewing.

How unusual at 6.30 a.m. He could not believe it would be Elijah, and with the bedroom still in darkness, and a lump of blankets in the bed, he could not make out whether or not Kathy was there. He was certainly not about to reach over to check and risk touching her, for that would only upset her if, in fact, she was.

Entering the kitchen and finding his wife there, albeit a very unwell, pale and thin version of her, was quite puzzling, to say the least. She had not been up with him in the morning since Angelina died. What on earth possessed her to start now, he could not imagine. He had got rather used to his mornings alone, and sometimes he even allowed himself the fantasy of Rosa being there, having made breakfast for him, wearing something silky and lacy and beautiful as she met him with passionate kisses in the kitchen.

He did not have any plans to leave his wife and family, but his fantasies seemed to keep him sane. They helped him through the hard parts of his life; they gave him a reprieve from the loneliness, the isolation, the cold, harsh reality that his marriage was at least in limbo, if not completely dead. He knew it was going to be a long time before he worked out what was happening in the family, and he was not willing to cross any lines before that.

But still, those fantasies about the beautiful, Italian Rosa were helping him through his days. And of course, there was the actual time spent with her, and how wonderful those hours were. Being together was so uncomplicated, so easy. Just talk of dreams and wishes and plans and ideas. Sharing joys and interests and learning of new ones. There was no work involved. There was no effort. It was just so simple.

And today, Robert and Rosa were going to listen to a barbershop quartet in the park at lunch time. He could not wait. But now, with Kathy having got up with him, he had to wonder what that meant. Was it just that she couldn't sleep? Could it be that she was trying to start anew? No, it couldn't be that. It didn't make sense. It must have been that she couldn't sleep. But from what she had said to him when he appeared in the kitchen, it almost sounded like she had got up and made the coffee specifically because of him.

Well, he wasn't going to let it bother him. He was just going to carry on as usual, and see what happened at home. For now, he was going to be excited about his wonderful lunch in the park with Rosa.

Kathy had been watching from the kitchen window as Robert's car headed down the drive and disappeared into the lane, hidden by the walls of trees that lined it. She had been disconnected from her feelings for her family for so long, it was painful to even consider the state that she was in. She did not know how she was going to get back to who she used to be, or if that was even possible. She had no idea where to begin with her boys, her husband, or even herself. She was a mess. A complete and absolute mess.

It was a beautiful day. The sun was just rising, the birds were singing, there was a whole world out there, waiting for her to taste it, experience it, enjoy it. And although the idea wafted through her weary brain long enough for her to recognize that it was a good thing, Kathy felt completely overwhelmed with all the problems she had to overcome. She did not know where to start. There were too many places, too many problems. She felt like a little child, staring at a huge table full of food and being told that she must eat every bit of it.

After a more positive start to her day than she'd had in months, in looking at all the harsh realities of her life and her family, suddenly, she felt as though there was no point in beginning to fix anything. She could never possibly accomplish all she would need to do in order to put things right. And the urge to go back to bed was just too tempting to resist it.

After a busy morning with patients and surgery, Robert met Rosa at the park. This was another unspoken rule; they never met at the hospital in order to reduce the possibility of people gossiping, and exposing the fact that they were spending time together. Always they made their plans to meet elsewhere, neither of them ever feeling a need to explain. It was just another way that the whole relationship with Rosa was so simple and uncomplicated. Robert had to admit it; he was falling in love, but he told himself that he was falling in love with the fantasy, since he did not really know the woman. He only knew a part of the woman. But he truly loved that part. And falling in love with a fantasy could not be dangerous. Or so he thought.

It was a perfect day; the sky was blue, there was not a cloud to be seen. There was only the slightest breeze on this beautiful late summer day. Rosa had brought a picnic basket filled with crusty French bread, and cheeses: smoked Gouda, a chunk of Havarti, and another of German butter cheese. There was a bowl of strawberries, a bunch of crisp, green grapes, and a bottle of lusty, rich red wine.

Sprawled out on a red and white checked blanket, Robert was once again impressed when Rosa brought crystal wine glasses, china plates and silver cutlery for the picnic, as she always did for such events. Being with Rosa was like being in a movie. She was always dressed so beautifully, in wonderful vibrant colours, flaming crimson, or indigo, brilliant blues or fuchsia. Her nails were always done to perfection, and the colour on her full and inviting lips always matched them.

Her voice was soft and soothing, her accent romantic and intriguing. Looking into her beautiful brown eyes, so large and warm, Robert felt as though he were falling. Rosa's dark hair, like waves and curls of silk, fell softly around her face, and Robert always felt compelled to push it away ever so gently with a fingertip, which he would then use to trace the outline of her neck.

And sometimes, Robert would lean over and kiss her, just there, in that wonderful place between her ear and her shoulder, her head tilted the other way, exposing this sweet and vulnerable place. And he would kiss her ever so gently, delicately, his fingers lightly running up and down the length of her arm.

One day, Robert could not stop there. He looked into those incredible, liquid, brown, velvety eyes, and suddenly, he was overcome with emotion. He kissed her hard, full on her mouth, passionately, as if every feeling he had ever experienced had been locked away forever, and had come rushing out in a flood.

And she had kissed him back, her hand on the back of his head as she pulled him closer to her. Robert held her, his right hand in the small of her back, drawing her near, his left hand running through her hair as he kissed her with a fire and an intensity that surprised both of them.

So far, Robert and Rosa had managed to keep their relationship from crossing a particular line, but it was becoming increasingly difficult. The more time they spent together, the more their passion for each other grew. It had taken on a life of its own, and demanded attention, whether or not it was appropriate.

His last afternoon patient gone, Robert closed the door to his office and crossed the room to his comfortable leather chair. Leaning back and swinging one leg up across the corner of his desk, he thought back over the events of the day. It had begun with Kathy's puzzling appearance in the kitchen that morning, Robert found himself remembering when his passion for her had been like that. Closing his eyes for just a moment, he was beginning to recall how it felt to be very much in love with his wife, to feel alive and excited at the thought of being with her. It was a crushing blow to face the reality of what their marriage had become, and to understand that he no longer felt the same kind of love and desire for Kathy that he had in the past. It was in this moment that he first understood just how serious the problems were, and he knew that his marriage really might be over.

It surprised him to find that he felt both fear and relief at the idea of no longer being married to Kathy. This was something that he would never have imagined just a few short months ago.

Pushing aside the possibilities for the future, he comforted himself with the knowledge that at the very least, he was still able to remember how it used to be.

And given the state of things between them, that in itself was quite an accomplishment. He was certain that many husbands would have allowed themselves a lot more freedom with Rosa than he had done, not that it made it okay that he was involved with her at all; he was well aware that this was not an appropriate situation.

Well, there was no point getting in a knot about one morning and a pot of coffee. It might have just been a sleepless night for his wife. It didn't have to mean anything more than that. And he'd had more than enough disappointment in recent years to last about seventeen lifetimes. And right now, he simply could not cope with another major disappointment with Kathy, and he did not *want* to cope with one that meant losing Rosa.

With a heavy sigh and an even heavier heart, he got on with his paperwork.

Fourteen

Elijah was tired. With his family in pieces, he had been trying so hard to do even better at school than before (and he was already an excellent student), and of course, he had been holding things together at home. Every now and then, he got a glimpse of the dad he loved and missed, and they spent a little time together. Those occasions gave him the tiniest bit of hope for the future, and he clung to that hope like it was a thread thrown to a drowning child in icy waters, desperate and scrambling to hold onto life, without much hope of survival.

And Elijah barely recognized James any more. He knew something was really wrong there; James was hardly ever home, and when he was, he was either too loud and too smiley, or too sullen and moody. Elijah was afraid that James had got into drugs, but he could not believe that his brother would actually try them. Their father was a doctor. Surely, he would know if that's what was going on. Wouldn't he?

Elijah said nothing, and just watched and waited to see what would happen next.

His mother had also changed since around the time of James's birthday. She had become even more quiet, if that was possible, at least when anyone was else was around. He was certain he could hear her talking to herself in other rooms when she was alone, but as soon as he or anyone else entered, she was instantly silent.

What was particularly odd was that when he heard her speaking, she sounded happy, like she was chatting away with someone, having a nice little visit. And one day, that thought brought him to a horrible possibility. What if his mother was talking to Angelina in 'the birthday way'? Elijah had never believed what Mummy had said that day; he believed that she was just pretending that Angelina was alive, and that was not at all the same as talking to her and knowing that she was dead.

It must be that, or why else would she stop talking as soon as someone joined her? And why would she sound so happy if she was talking to Angelina, knowing she is dead? He talked to Angelina all the time, but it was different from how he had spoken with her when she was alive.

Elijah was carrying the weight of the world on his shoulders. His mother was in a bad way, as near as he could tell. His father was hardly ever home, and when he was, he was busy with house and yard things, and rarely spent any time with the boy any more. As for James, he had all but vanished from their lives.

So Elijah just did his best to be a perfect student, and to be a good lad at home, as he tried to be the glue that held these broken people together individually, never mind as a family. But the strain was getting to be too much. He feared something or someone was going to break entirely. And there wasn't anything he could do about it. His helplessness spurred him on, frantically trying to find ways to make everything better.

He was doing more than most kids his age could manage. He was 11, his birthday having come and gone in the early fall with a very quiet celebration in his family. He had not had any interest in having a party with friends and all of that. He did not enjoy bringing people to his home any more; it was not a happy place. It was not at all what it used to be, not even remotely.

Mrs. Scott was his teacher this year, and she had been asking a lot of questions lately; she said she was very concerned about him. She thought he was looking too pale and tired, and that he was too quiet, maybe depressed. He knew that she was right, and being autumn, well, it was getting too close to Christmas, and this was likely to create even more trouble within the family. And Heaven knew they didn't need any more of *that*.

Elijah wanted to celebrate Christmas, but he was certain that no one else in the family did. Usually by this time, they were well into discussing plans and gifts, and this year, the word had not crossed the lips of anyone in the Lane household.

With the terribly painful anniversary looming for a family that was already very distressed, Elijah well understood why he wasn't looking or feeling his best, but he was still hopeful that the situation would improve. He had heard many people say that the first year, and all the 'first anniversaries' are the worst after someone dies. So Elijah was expecting that after New Year's Eve, the last of those awful 'firsts', his family would finally start to recover. Or at least, he was hoping with the desperation of someone hanging by his fingertips from the crumbling edge of a cliff.

He told Mrs. Scott some of this, hoping that she would understand, as Mrs. Robinson had done the previous year. When she mentioned wanting to talk to his parents about him, he reassured her that he was all right (and of course, he wasn't, not really, but he was still managing to cope with things). He realized that he was going to have to put on a happier face at school, and try harder to cover what was going on at home, or she was going to be calling his parents. And the last thing they needed was one more worry.

So Elijah tried harder to prove to Mrs. Scott that he was really okay.

And he spent lots of time talking to Angelina. He was more certain all the time that she really was there and listening to him; sometimes he even felt like maybe she was answering. It gave him so much comfort to believe that she was still with him, at least sometimes.

After understanding how her parents and James were too lost to be able to communicate with her, or even to hear or feel her, Angelina focused on practicing to communicate with Elijah. She was surprised at how much energy it took on both sides, and had learned a lot about how other life events can get in the way of people receiving messages from The Other Side. Her family certainly had a lot going on, and the only one who was spiritually oriented, and therefore had any real hope of connecting with her, was Elijah.

But it was well into autumn, and the Little Angel could see that her family's situation was getting critical. Poor Elijah! He was trying so hard to hold everything together! Angelina was stunned to see what had happened to everyone else, but she also knew that each of them had lessons to learn, and there was not a lot that anyone else could do. At least she could offer comfort to Elijah, if he could just hear her messages!

Elijah was very grateful for his spiritual beliefs; they had carried him through this terrible time and many others. He had begun to realize that the family's difficulties did not begin when Angelina died. There had been a lot of heartache and pain long before that happened. And he was very grateful that he believed his sister was listening to him; if not for her, his life would have been unbearably lonely in the past ten months since her death. Well, it was nice to have Frank, too, but as much as he loved the little cat, she was no match for Angelina. He remembered when his mother first found out that she was expecting his little sister, and how he knew then that he had a very strong connection with her. It had begun before her birth, and only strengthened throughout her life and after her death. And that connection gave Elijah comfort that he could not find anywhere else.

With Christmas approaching, Elijah's conflict about it grew daily. He wanted to discuss it with his family, but was afraid to cause more upset. But time waits for no one, and he had to make a decision about it soon.

One night in early November, Elijah had lain awake in bed, chewing on this issue for a long time before finally drifting off to sleep. And while he slept, he dreamed of Angelina. He could see his sister so clearly, and she was telling him that they must have Christmas. And in the dream, Elijah argued with her, telling her about what the family would say. But she would not listen. She just kept telling him that they must have Christmas.

In the morning, Elijah woke feeling tired and restless, and the dream was nagging at him. It bothered him for much of the day, but by the evening, he had managed to put it out of his head, deciding that his original choice was the best one. His family was in pieces; things were worse than ever. Mentioning Christmas at this point might be all that was needed for them to completely shatter.

But as the days passed, the dream kept popping into Elijah's memory with increasing frequency. And then he had it again one night, only Angelina's voice was louder this time. She was much more insistent in the dream, and again, he was trying to explain to her why it was not a good idea. But she would not listen.

And just like before, Elijah chewed on the dream for some time afterward, uncertain about whether he should say anything to his family. But as he watched things crumbling around him at home, he was more convinced than ever that he should remain silent on the subject of Christmas.

Elijah was certainly right about things crumbling around him, and he was right about the response that he would have got, had he mentioned the notion of celebrating Christmas that year. Certainly, James was in no mood for it. In fact, even James himself had no idea that he could reach such extreme levels of rage. He was pretty certain that he could not possibly get any more angry than he already was, but he was wrong. The closer it got to December, the more he stewed and boiled, but he never spoke of his feelings to anyone.

Of course, he did not really need to say a word. Everyone who spent any time with him could see what was happening; but no one knew why. Well, yes, Billy and Mike knew, but they most certainly never dared mention Angelina or anything to do with her. So everyone else at Mad Dog's or on the drug route only knew that this was one terrifying, intimidating and potentially extremely volatile, lethal young man. They did not need to understand his rage to respect it, and everyone tried to steer clear of being on the receiving end of it.

Even Bull, Crazy and the other bikers kept their distance. That kid was a walking time bomb and everyone around him knew it. Funny how he didn't seem to know it himself, though. He had got so used to choking on his feelings, this had just become part of who he was.

It was late November when Mike, James and Billy headed out to Mad Dog's one Saturday evening. It was cold and snowy, and there were Christmas decorations popping up already. Many of the houses and businesses that they passed were lit up with twinkling coloured lights. Father Christmases and reindeer, snowmen and wreaths were screaming out at James, taunting, mocking, tormenting him. Reaching for the volume control in Billy's car, he cranked the stereo even louder, sinking into his anger while a thousand screams ripped through his soul.

Using the back entrance as they always did, the boys saw Mad Dog in the kitchen, his large belly protruding under his filthy apron, a cigarette hanging out of his mouth as he stood at the stove, frying some greasy thing or other for a customer. They called out to him and put up a hand as a sort of wave on their way through, and he smiled and nodded in their direction, squinting against the smoke that was snaking its way into his eyes.

James and Billy had been at Mad Dog's the night before, and there had been nothing out of the ordinary, but on that Saturday evening, they arrived to find a bit of Christmas decorating in the shabby little pub. As they entered and saw this, Mike and Billy caught the look in James's eye, but neither said a word to him or to each other. And both prepared for the fallout.

Crazy wasn't anywhere in sight, but Bull and a few of his pals were there. The boys pulled up chairs and sat next to Bull, who offered them each a cigarette. Thanking him, they accepted the offer. A book of matches with Mad Dog's advertising on it was lying on the table. James scooped it up and lit their smokes before shoving the matches in his coat pocket. Finally, Mad Dog came out of the kitchen and returned to his place behind the bar. Billy went and got a round for the group.

James was doing his best not to pay attention to the Christmas decorations, realizing that he was going to be faced with an awful lot more of them in the coming weeks, never mind years. It had been much easier for him to forget Angelina's death and all the repercussions when there weren't any Christmas reminders anywhere. He had not even considered that this was going to be an issue; he had got so good at blocking out the whole matter, he had not stopped to think about the fact that there would be decorations everywhere before long.

Bull noticed something different in James's face that night, and wondered whether he should mention it. He was a mountain of a man, and certainly was not physically threatened by James, but his hesitation about bringing up a potentially painful subject was more of a respectful thing than anything. He still did not know what it was that made this kid be the way he was, but he understood that there was something that had got him so full of rage that he was scary for most people to deal with. He had a soft spot for the kid, and felt rather protective of him, almost fatherly, in fact.

Bull had never had any of his own kids. Well, at least, not that he knew about! He had always been careful about such things; he knew he was too wild and free to be tied down to a woman and kids.

But he liked other people's kids. And he surely liked this one. It had been many months since he had met James, and instantly, he had taken a liking to the lad, despite his foul temper, despite the rage that was obviously simmering and sometimes boiling just beneath the surface. He had tried to teach James lots of tricks to keep himself safe with drugs, with bikers, with people in general. Sure, some people would laugh about his feelings of protectiveness toward James, while at the same time having been the person who turned the kid onto coke and crack. He never professed to be perfect. And besides, he was sure the kid was headed there anyway. The least he could do is try to teach him to be a little more street-wise so he didn't end up dead.

He liked the other two kids all right, too. That Mike kid, boy, he was sure in a mess with his family. He never said much about it, just that the old man was shacked up with some young woman, and the kid's mother was giving him all kinds of grief about it every time he went to visit his dad. He was stuck in the middle of all that, and every now and then, he came along with James and Billy for a bit of a night out. He didn't seem to have the same sense of adventure that his mates had; he wasn't too likely to get into much trouble in his life, at least not without a whole lotta help. Bull often wondered just what Mike thought about this place, these people, their lives. He was pretty sure that the kid had grown up in a whole different kind of atmosphere than the one in *this* joint.

And Billy. He was pretty much okay. Probably nothing that kid wouldn't try if he thought there was a little fun in it. Still, despite how nuts he could get, Bull thought there was still an element of sensibility about him. Sure, he drank or did some drugs, and then drove home later, but at least he usually waited a while, or would at least limit what he had. Most of the bozos in that place, and every other pub he had ever been in, would just slug it back and get behind the wheel. Sorta had to respect the skinny little guy for that.

He and James had quite the little business going. Bull was rather impressed with the fact that they had done so well for so long, and had avoided any contact with police for all these months. For their ages, that was really something. They must have been doing a pretty amazing job, not to get caught.

Yep, there was all kinds of stuff to like and respect about these guys. If only he knew what it was about James, though. He was the one that Bull especially liked and cared about. He was the one that Bull wished he could help. But he had absolutely no experience with kids, and hadn't a clue what he could or should say. But he thought it was time to consider it. Maybe there was some way he could help this kid. 'Cause if someone didn't, Bull was sure that something really awful was going to happen. And soon.

The boys hung out for a while that evening, joking and talking with Bull and his buddies. Well, James wasn't doing much joking or talking, but he was trying to act as though nothing was different. To the unobservant onlooker, he probably seemed as quiet and angry as he always did. But to someone like

Bull, who liked James and who knew him as much as anyone could, it was clear that something was really wrong.

And because Bull noticed that James was different, Bull was a little different, too, that night. He was a little more fatherly with James. He stretched out an arm behind the boy, laying his hand on James's shoulder in a sort of parental manner. He looked the boy straight in the eye a time or two, and without wanting to come right out and be specific about his concern, he asked meaningful questions in a meaningful way. Like, "How *are* you?" with an intent look to go with it. Or "You know, James, if you need anything..."

It seemed that for a while, James was kind of taken aback with the changes in Bull that night. He didn't really seem to know what to do with all of that. And so, as with most things at that time in his life, James did nothing. After all this time, desperately needing someone to throw him a lifeline, finally, someone had done it. And he hadn't a clue how to take hold of it. Not a clue.

"Hey, Mike," said Billy, "James and I have to do our routes. You wanna come along or you wanna wait here?"

Mike considered his options for a moment. It was never much fun to go on drug runs with his mates. He was either stuck sitting in the car waiting while they went into each of the homes on their routes, or he had to endure going with them. Neither idea was particularly appealing that night.

"Bull, you gonna be here a while?" asked Mike.

"Sure, kid. You can hang with us if you want."

"Okay, yeah, I'll stay here then," Mike said as he turned to Billy.

"Hey, James, are you about ready to go to work? Got everything?" Billy asked.

"Just getting myself stocked up," replied James while Bull was handing over rocks and powder, based on James's usual orders from his customers.

Once the two were ready to go, they put on their coats, lit cigarettes and headed out the back door, saying, "See ya in a couple hours, guys!" And with that, the door slammed behind them.

It had continued to snow for a while after they had gone into the pub, but had stopped by the time the boys left. They brushed off the windows and got into the car, shivering in the cold.

Summer was so much nicer; what a treat to just get in and go.

The two had got pretty good at their route, and they could get through it rather quickly after having done it so many times. Sometimes there were changes, a few adds, or a rare drop, but they kept up really well and were usually back at Mad Dog's within about two hours of leaving.

Everyone at the bar was also pretty impressed with how well these young guys handled their business. They were very strict about not handing over any goodies without being paid first. They had been taught from the beginning that if you do that once, you will be expected to do it again and again, and before long, you're out of business because your supplier will want his money, and you won't ever get it from crackheads if you let them off the hook even once.

Everyone on their route knew that whatever they were selling, it had to be paid for before it would be handed over. Yep, these two entrepreneurs were doing pretty darned well!

James and Billy had even got used to seeing the really creepy, dirty places, especially the ones that smelled bad, or the ones with hookers or other people lying around, screaming in withdrawal, begging for just one more hit. They were always careful to leave their shoes on in those places, never wanting to step on any used needles. Besides, they never knew when they might need to run.

On this particular Saturday night, it was the same as always, and the one thing that made James particularly happy was that at least at these crack houses, no one was bothering to decorate for Christmas. They drove up an alley, and the two walked up to the back door of the first house, the one where there were always hookers lying around in varying stages of undress, some flying, some desperate to be, the place that smelled of stale urine and was about the most repulsive on their route, so it was always good to get it over with first. Everything looked and smelled better after that place.

When they arrived, their customer, known only as 'Rider', was looking nervous. He was pacing back and forth across the kitchen as the boys came in through the porch.

"Oh, man, I'm so glad you guys are here. Been waitin' a long time," he said, apparently in pretty serious need of a little pharmaceutical assistance, as far as James and Billy could see.

"Yeah, you ain't lookin' too good, mate. No sweat, we can fix you up right away," said James. "Where's the cash?"

Rider looked away from the boys, and eyes downcast said, "Sorry, mate, I ain't got your money this time. Couldja just give me a little for tonight and I'll get it to you by Monday?" His eyes had that pained, anxious look that they had seen so often on their customer's faces.

"Sorry, man," said James, "You know the drill. If we don't take back the cash to our supplier, then we're in it, ya know? Wish we could help you, but we just can't. Do ya have any on you at all?"

"No, man. Nothin'. I'm pretty much cleaned right out," Rider said. "Please, you guys, just a little, just this once?" he pleaded.

"Aw, man, c'mon, don't do this to us. It's not up to us!" said James. "We're just the guys in the middle, and if we go back with no drugs and no money, we're seriously in trouble. Tell ya what, we'll come back in a day or two, just tell us when you think you'll have some cash."

"That's not good enough!" cried Rider, his eyes growing a little wilder by the minute, and he paced a little faster. "You don't understand! It was a really bad day, man. I can't wait!"

"Well, I'm sorry, buddy, but you're gonna have to. We'll come back tomorrow, okay?" said James. And turning to Billy, he continued. "C'mon, Billy, let's go."

As the boys turned and left the porch, they could still hear the pleas of a desperate addict, calling after them, begging them to reconsider. Well, truth be told, there wasn't any other kind of addict. It wasn't the first time they had heard such pleas, and they were certain it wouldn't be the last. All they did know was that it was guys like Rider who kept them in business. And it wouldn't have mattered if they had got out of this line of work; someone else would always be there to do it. This is how they justified what they were doing; it was how they could go home and sleep at night without giving their customers another thought.

They made their way back to the alley, and just as they neared the car, James shook his head and turned to

Billy. "Poor bloke. Man, that must suck, being in that kind of shape."

All of a sudden, the boys heard several loud cracking sounds at the same time as they felt something hot pierce their bodies. It took a few seconds for each boy to realize that he had been shot a few times, the bullets ripping through their flesh, throwing the boys to the ground. As they lay there, terrified and in shock, feeling the life pouring out of them and onto the snow, they wondered how long it would be before they died.

Angelina had witnessed this, and horrified, raced to find Elijah, who was reading in his room. It was getting on for a Saturday evening and he was supposed to be in bed. Well, in bed he was, but not yet asleep. Kathy was watching something on television, and Robert was out somewhere, presumbly at his office, although it was awfully late for that. Sometimes he had emergencies, maybe that's what was keeping him.

Angelina sat on the bed in front of Elijah and did her very best to send urgent messages to let him know that James was in trouble. It didn't take long for Elijah to feel her in the room, and he also noticed that it was different this time. Usually, there was just a sweet, quiet presence that he was certain was his little sister. But this time, the hair on his arms and on the back of his neck stood up and he got the distinct impression that something was wrong. He was unable to determine where or with whom, but he was certain that he was being given a message about bad news.

Of course, with his worries about James, he had to wonder whether something had happened to his brother. He didn't know what to do. He couldn't very well go to his mother with 'a feeling'. After all, what could she do with that? He supposed that all anyone could really do was wait and hope that if there *was* a problem, it would be quickly resolved and James would be okay.

Elijah began to speak to Angelina. "Is that you? Are you here? Are you trying to tell me that something's wrong?" he asked.

"Yes, oh, yes, Elijah! I am! Please! Try to hear me! You have to get help for James!" Angelina was concentrating as hard as she could to try to get this message to her brother.

"Angelina! Try harder! You must be trying to tell me something! What is it??!" Elijah squeezed his eyes shut and tried to be more open to receiving messages from the Little Angel.

Angelina pictured James and Billy lying in the snow. She tried to send a picture of the name of the village, and the boys' location, but it was a lot for her to manage under the circumstances.

Elijah concentrated as hard as he could. He thought he saw what looked like two people lying in the snow in a very dark place by a fence. But that was all he could see. And he was certain that one of them was James, not from what he could see, but from what he was being made to feel.

While Angelina tried unsuccessfully to get help, Rider came out of the house after he saw James and Billy fall to the ground. Sneaking up close to them, he heard nothing out of either boy, and neither one was moving. There wasn't much light in the alley, just a little coming from kitchen windows or the occasional garage or gate lamp, but it was enough to see rapidly pooling blood under both of the young men.

Rider poked at both of them with his boot. Neither boy moved. Quickly, he dug in their pockets, emptying the contents on the ground beside their bodies, taking their wallets and removing all the drugs and cash that he could find. Plucking Billy's keys out of the snow, he jumped in behind the wheel of the old car and took off, knowing that someone would have heard the shots, and the police would be there shortly. But at least with the car and their wallets gone and no identification, Rider had a bit of a head start.

Fifteen

Angelina left Elijah and went back to check on James and Billy. But by the time she got there, she saw Billy coming through the bright, warm light and crossing over to The Other Side, where he was met by several people whom she did not know.

She watched for a few moments, and saw that he was settling in, and then went to see what was happening with James. A police car was there, and Angelina could hear an ambulance on the way, but it was still a bit of a distance from where the shooting occurred. As she watched, praying that her brother would be all right, suddenly, James's spirit rose up out of his body and slowly drifted toward her. He was looking around, surprised and dazed, not quite understanding what was happening.

James saw Angelina above him, and at first, he was puzzled, but then he smiled as he realized what was happening. He was so happy to see his sister, and dying was very peaceful; there was no need to be upset. The paramedics had arrived and had begun thumping on James's chest, and zapping him with their paddles. He continued to look down at them while he drifted up toward his sister, the light around him growing brighter and warmer.

Angelina turned and saw her two Grannies and her Grandpa there, and the other friends and relatives who had come to welcome her when she crossed over, and she realized that it must be James's turn, too. She felt so sad for her parents and Elijah; this was going to be such a terrible blow.

The paramedics were still pounding on James's chest, and they had a little bag over his mouth, trying to get air into him. But his heart was still not beating on its own. They were working hard to revive the young man, hoping to keep his blood circulating and his brain oxygenated. But with that dark pool around him, there wasn't much blood left in his body.

And still James watched, feeling more and more peaceful as he drifted heavenward, toward his little sister.

It was not long after James and Billy left Mad Dog's that a policeman walked in. Now that was a rare occurrence; they usually left that place alone. No one there ever gave them any trouble, and they didn't see much need to go in there and clean house on a regular basis. They were happy to let sleeping dogs lie.

The boys had only been gone about 45 minutes, when the officer came in, calling out that there had been an incident and he needed some help in identifying two teenaged boys. As he described James and Billy, and mentioned their location, everyone knew immediately who they were. Bull and Mike rose from their chairs, while Mad Dog came quickly from behind the bar, all of them asking what was going on.

"Sounds like our mates, James and Billy, sir," said Mike, terror rising in his throat as he spoke.

"Does anyone here know how to get in touch with the parents?" asked the officer.

"I do," said Mike. "They're my best mates. Please, tell me what's going on!" he begged.

"I'm sorry, son, but there's been a shooting," was the startling reply.

"A shooting??! What are you talking about? Where? How are they? What's happened?" Mike felt weak in the knees and sank into his chair. Bull sat down beside him and put his arm around the boy, trying to calm him. Everyone in the pub was stunned. Questions erupted from every corner of the room; no one was unaffected by the shocking news.

"We don't know what happened yet. It looks like a mugging," replied the officer. "We found a book of matches beside one of them, matches from this place. That was the only ID at the scene. When we arrived, neither had a pulse or a heartbeat. Paramedics weren't there yet last I heard, but both boys were shot a few times, looks like a fair bit of damage, and an awful lot of blood loss. I'm sorry to have to tell you about this." The officer paused, staring at the floor, and giving everyone a few moments to absorb what he had said.

Putting a hand on Mike's shoulder, the officer leaned down and gently asked for names and phone numbers so he could get in touch with the parents.

It was getting quite late for the phone to be ringing. Kathy was mildly annoyed, but then realized it might be James or Robert -- more likely Robert, since they barely saw or heard from James any more.

She was wrong on both counts. It was a police officer, telling her about James having been shot. And worse, he had been found without a pulse. He said that although paramedics were working on him while he was being transported to the hospital, they were struggling to get a heartbeat. It did not appear that they would be able to resuscitate him. He had lost an awful lot of blood, and no one was sure how long he had been lying there in that condition. His friend was dead, having received a fatal shot in the back of his head, and the parents had just been notified.

Kathy dropped the phone and collapsed into a chair by the bed. She must be dreaming, this could not be real. How much was one family supposed to take? Where was Robert? She had her suspicions but she could not think about that just then. What was she to do?

Elijah had heard the phone ring, and given the premonition he'd had, he just knew it was bad news about James. Throwing back the blankets, he stepped into his slippers and grabbed his bathrobe from the foot of the bed. Wrapping it around himself, he crept out of his room, and made his way to his mother's side. He found her slumped in a chair in her room, hysterically crying, the telephone on the floor beside her.

He could hear someone on the other end of the line, and picking up the phone, he asked the person to wait a moment, please.

Elijah knelt down in front of his mother and very gently asked her what had happened. Kathy realized that with Robert away, she had no choice but to pull herself together and deal with this. Wiping her face with the backs of her hands, she took a deep breath and hurriedly told the young boy what had happened. Taking the phone from him, she apologized to the officer and asked which hospital they were planning to use.

Unfortunately, the closest one to James at that time was not the one where Robert practiced. It would have been nice to have James in a place which offered some familiarity, some measure of comfort in that regard. And especially if they were just going to receive confirmation of what the policeman basically told her.

She could not remember much about the call, or even whether she hung up, until she looked at the phone and saw that it was, indeed, back on its cradle. Noticing Elijah still sitting on the floor in front of her, his eyes brimming with tears, she told him to get dressed as quickly as possible. They had to leave right away.

Once the boy was out of the room, Kathy rang Robert's mobile. She knew there was a good chance that he was with Rosa, or possibly some other woman. But she had no choice but to call.

Robert and Rosa had spent a few delightful hours together that evening. They had attended an art exhibition, after which they made their way to one of their favourite little inns, out in the middle of nowhere. It was hundreds of years old, and with its thick, stone walls and its wonderful thatched roof and ceiling beams, it had all the charm anyone could possibly want for a romantic little hideout.

They were happy to have found a table for two in a private corner of the pub, right beside the open fireplace. Ancient pots of copper and brass and other interesting bits and pieces hung from the mantle, or were stood on the stone hearth. The fire popped and crackled, and cast a soft and lovely glow upon the couple in the dimly lit room. Celtic music played quietly in the background, adding to the already warm and cozy atmosphere of this beautiful old inn. The two felt as though they were in a world all their own.

They had enjoyed a wonderful, leisurely meal, while sharing a bottle of their favourite red wine, chatting about the art exhibition and a million other delightful topics.

Rosa's eyes, so dark and deep, sparkled and danced in the firelight, her lovely, olive skin making Robert ache to touch it; his fingers longed to stroke it ever so gently, to feel its creamy smooth texture beneath them. He had not thought it possible for her to be any more beautiful than she already was, but there, by the soft light of the fire, he knew he was wrong. She was far more stunning than he had ever realized. He had come to know her soul, and at that moment, he understood that he had to know her body, too. He wanted to explore every part of this woman, wanted to taste her skin, to feel her respond to his touch, to hear her catch her breath as his hands searched for the most sensitive places. He longed to hear her moans and whispers, urging him on, begging him not to stop.

And he knew from the look in her beautiful, sparkling eyes, that she wanted it, too.

Glancing at the antique grandfather clock in the corner, he realized that Elijah should be in bed. And knowing his wife, in all likelihood, she would be asleep, too. He was contemplating how to ask Rosa if she wanted to take a room upstairs when his mobile rang, a sharp intrusion into their private and perfect world. It shattered the peace, the silence, and worst of all, the fantasy.

Robert considered not answering, but with the late hour, he realized that it must be some sort of emergency. Hoping that it was one that could be handled in a phone call, he flipped up the cover of his mobile and saw that it was someone from home who was ringing him.

Rosa did not need to hear the words; the look on his face told her exactly who it was on the phone. Making it easier for him to answer, she excused herself and went to the ladies' room.

Robert pressed the 'talk' button and said, "Hello?"

There was a brief pause before he heard Kathy's strained voice on the other end of the line. "Robert, I don't know how to tell you this. Are you driving?"

"No, I'm not," he replied. "What's wrong?"

There was another pause, and suddenly, Kathy burst into sobs. Struggling to get the words out, she told Robert in fits and starts the horrific news about James.

Robert's blood ran cold. After learning what Kathy had been told, he asked where James was being taken. Just as she was giving him the name of the hospital, Rosa returned to the table, but hung back to give Robert some privacy.

Instantly, Rosa could see that the colour had drained from his face. She had never seen him look like this before, and knew that something really terrible had happened. She heard him say something about meeting the other person, presumably his wife, and knew that they would be leaving momentarily. Reaching for her coat from the rack nearby, she could hear that the call was ending, and she waited to see whether Robert would share what was going on.

The call had been their first blast of reality. It had intruded on their perfect, fantasy relationship, and there was no turning back. The time had come for Robert to break the unspoken rule. As he hurried to put some cash on the table and put his coat on, he told Rosa very briefly about Angelina, about Kathy's behaviour for nearly a year, and then the news about James. He wanted her to understand that Kathy was very fragile, and that she was going to need him now like never before.

"I'm so sorry, my dear Rosa, but I may not be able to call you for a while," Robert apologized.

"I want to go with you to the hospital, Robert. I can't stand the idea of you being there without someone to support you."

"Thank you, Rosa, but how can you be there for me when..." His voice trailed off, both of them knowing what he meant; there was no need for him to finish the question.

"Robert, I do not have to be right there in the room with you for you to feel my support," she explained, while they hurried outside to the car park.

"But I don't want to put you through all of this. It's never been part of our -- our --" Robert replied, struggling to find the appropriate word. Rosa stopped walking. With her hand on his arm, she turned him to face her. Reaching up, she laid her fingers very gently on his lips.

Rosa gazed up at him with an intent look that he was seeing in her eyes for the first time. "It is true," she said, "reality has never been a part of this. But that choice is no longer ours."

She was right, and he knew it. But they had no time for this discussion just now; he had to get to the hospital. Pulling away from her grasp, he headed toward his car, saying, "You're right, Rosa, but you don't need this."

"Do not presume to tell me what I need, Robert," she replied gently, but with conviction. "Much more importantly right now, what about what *you* need?"

Robert stopped in his tracks, dumbfounded. Rosa got it. She knew. She knew every bit of it. He had always been the person upon whom others leaned, the one who was needed, whether by his family, his friends, or his patients. Sure, previously, he had been able to lean on Kathy in many ways for a long time, but even then, he could only go so far. Since he was a boy, he had always stepped into roles of strength and support, never asking for anything in return.

Robert could not deny that it would be a help to him, knowing that Rosa was at the hospital that night, even if he could not actually communicate with her while Kathy was present. For almost a year, there had been no one for him to lean on at all, and it was a year in which he could certainly have stood the support. Heaven knew he really needed someone now. Certain that Kathy would not be able to provide any comfort or consolation, sure that she could not be a source of strength for him, he was relieved to have Rosa nearby. He thanked her, and they got into their cars. Rosa followed him, and once they reached the hospital car park, she was sure to keep her distance.

The police were crawling all over the murder scene. They had a large section of the alley cordoned off, and it was being given a thorough going-over, looking for any evidence that might point the police in the direction of the killer or killers. It appeared that the boys had been mugged; their wallets were gone, and there was no other immediately obvious reason for two teenagers to be shot in an alley. But what were they doing there? It seemed that they were shot from behind. The police could only guess at the trajectory of the bullets at that point, but it seemed that they might have come from the back of one of the houses.

Police photographers were still getting shots of Billy, after which he would be put into a body bag and loaded into the coroner's wagon. James was on his way to the hospital, since paramedics had been able to re-start his heart. But it wasn't going well. His heart kept stopping, and it was taking longer and longer to get it started again each time.

Billy was settling in on The Other Side, and he smiled when he saw the Little Angel there, too, along with grandparents and others who were apparently waiting to welcome James. Looking down, he saw his friend drifting closer to the beautiful, bright light, while people below kept working on his body in an ambulance, and then in an operating room, trying to make his heart beat. James, Billy, the Little Angel and the others with them heard the doctors commenting on how it was time to stop trying, saying that it had been too long, and he was dead.

Finally, James reached the bright, warm light and started to make his way through it, coming nearer to the Little Angel, who held out her arms to welcome her big brother. They smiled at each other as he drifed closer. It was going to be so hard for Mummy and Daddy and Elijah, but if James was here, then it was meant to be, and someday, they would understand that.

Kathy was the first to arrive at the hospital. She was told that because her son's heart kept stopping, he was not a good candidate for surgery, which he desperately needed to prevent any more blood loss. As it was, his aorta had been nicked by one of the bullets, and he was bleeding to death. There was virtually no hope; there had been too much damage, combined with the blood loss, and death was inevitable.

Kathy was glad that Elijah was with her, although she was well aware that it was terrible for him to experience any of this. Although upon thinking about it, she knew him well enough to know that he would not want to be home alone at such a time. She was grateful for his company, especially since Robert was not yet there. The waiting was horrible anyway, but to have been alone would have been unbearable. Kathy was on very shaky ground, having just begun to look at what her life had become. She was a long way from being strong, and from being the kind of mother that Elijah deserved. She well knew that she had been leaning on him far too much, and because of his wise and spiritual nature, he had never complained, but rather, had taken on the burden willingly.

She looked down at Elijah, who was holding her hand. He looked so tired, and far older than his 11 years. It broke Kathy's heart to think of all he had endured in the past year. And even before that, if the truth be told. Kathy was starting to see that there were many issues which had been buried and unresolved for a very long time. She had no idea how she or her family would begin to wade through the muck that already existed.

And now there was this. And as far as the doctors were concerned, James had already died, and they were just trying to revive him, so far unsuccessfully.

Robert found Kathy and Elijah in the waiting room, which was quite full, as is usually the case on Saturday nights in hospital emergency rooms. Rosa waited down the hall for a few moments, and then took a seat amongst the others on the opposite side of the room. She picked up a magazine and began to flip through it, never once glancing in the direction of Robert or his family. It was rather awkward for him, seeing her there in the same room with Kathy, yet he also felt better, knowing there was someone there for him, and he appreciated her for it.

Robert got as much information as he could from Kathy, and then went to seek out any medical staff who had worked on James when he came in. He and his wife had countless questions about how this happened, as well as what his current status was.

Just after Robert left, a couple of detectives came to speak to Kathy. They told her all they knew, and asked a lot of questions in an effort to find out who did this to her son and to Billy.

It was impossible to believe that Billy was actually dead. Kathy and Robert had known Billy all of his life, having met his parents before he was born. The Lanes had been newcomers to the area, and Billy's family, who lived just up the road, had welcomed them upon their arrival. Close friendships had developed between the two families throughout their years as neighbours.

Billy was just two years older than James, and the boys had spent a lot of time together all their lives. In fact, Billy was the first friend James ever had. How bizarre that they should come to this end together.

The shock of that idea kept hitting Kathy over and over like a tidal wave. She was struggling to grasp the idea that Billy was actually dead and on his way to a morgue, and at the same time, was trying to understand James' situation. There was really very little hope, according to the doctors. So she prepared, as best she could, for the worst.

Robert finally tracked down some of the staff who had cared for James when he came in. The news was about as bad as it could be. Robert was told about the very unstable condition of James's heart, about his tremendous blood loss, and about the specific damage that was done as the bullets tore through his body. He was also told that they did not expect him to have made it this long, and it was extremely unlikely that he would survive the surgery -- that is, if they could stabilize him enough to operate at all. They were in the operating theatre, but his heart kept stopping and they were struggling to make any progress in repairing the damage to his body.

It was a crushing blow. There were no words to describe the shock, the horror, the anger, and countless other emotions that rolled through Robert as he stood, trying to digest the information that he had been given.

He wanted to go and assist the doctors, or at least watch the surgery. But the doctors refused to allow it; he was, understandably, far too upset. And besides, they reminded him that his wife and son were waiting for him, and they needed him.

Oh, for once in his life, could he please not hear about how someone needed him?! He felt as though he would explode just at that moment, but somehow, he managed to gather himself together, and go and see to Kathy and Elijah.

As he made his way through the hospital corridors, he decided to go and get some coffee for himself and Kathy, and a drink for Elijah. Off he went to the cafeteria. And what was it about hospitals and cafeterias anyway? There, as if she were waiting for him, was Rosa.

Because of the late hour, there weren't many people in the cafeteria. Not even any staff were out in the front at that moment, and being an unfamiliar hospital, Robert thought that it was safe for them to share a warm embrace. It was so good to hold her, and to know that she was offering her strength and support. It was wonderful to hold her and know that it was not because she needed him. It felt so good to know that if he had wanted to break down and cry right then and there, that would have been fine with her.

But of course, he did not do that. Instead, he just cherished the few moments that she held him, before he had to give her the dreadful update.

"You know, Rosa, all those years we knew we were probably going to lose

Angelina, and we thought that we were prepared for it, or at least, as much as we could have been. But we weren't. And sometimes, we thought it would have been better if she had just gone suddenly, if we had to lose her at all. But we were wrong about that, too. This is just so horrible! We've had no warning. Things have been such a mess, I'm not even sure of what were the last words I spoke to my son, or which day I last saw him!"

And with that, Robert broke down and did, in fact, cry, while Rosa just held him as they stood there in the cafeteria. There was nothing else she could do. No words would help. Nothing could save him from this unbearable pain.

After Robert had gone to find out anything he could about James, and after the detectives left, Kathy and Elijah were waiting for quite some time. Finally, after what seemed like days, a solemn-looking doctor appeared, calling for Mr. and Mrs. Lane. Kathy looked up at him, hoping for even a little good news, but upon seeing his expression, her face fell.

"Mrs. Lane," said the doctor as Kathy rose to meet him, "I'm Dr. Fortin. I've been with your son since he came in tonight. He's still in the operating theatre, and frankly, it's not going well. Why don't we go somewhere a little more private so I can tell you where things stand?" With that, he led her to a tiny room down the corridor, away from everyone else. Kathy knew what that meant. Those rooms were saved for the people who were about to hear the worst possible news.

After they were seated, he continued. "I have to tell you, we are really shocked that your son is still hanging on, although it truly is by a thread. He's suffered some pretty traumatic injuries."

The doctor gave the information to the distraught mother in little pieces. There was no easy way to say it, but at least he could give it a little at a time.

"One of the bullets tore through his right kidney and shattered it. We were unable to save it and it has been removed. Another bullet went through his left lung, which was collapsed, so we have inserted a chest tube."

Dr. Fortin paused once again, to give Kathy a chance to absorb what he had said. She surprised herself, and remained much more calm than she would have expected. Perhaps it was because she knew the worst was yet to come.

The doctor went on. "James's aorta was torn so he had significant blood loss. Now, we've repaired the damage to the aorta, but because of the severe hemorrhaging, he has suffered several heart attacks, which has damaged the heart muscle."

Kathy's face turned to a terrible ash gray. She was stunned to hear all of this, and felt as though she could not stand to hear any more. "Please! Give me a moment before you tell me any more!" she begged Dr. Fortin.

"Of course, I understand," he replied, his voice filled with compassion. As he looked deep into her eyes, Kathy could see that he was a very kind man, and she knew that she could trust him completely. He was one of those wonderful doctors who remembered the point of being a healer, and she would never forget him.

After a couple of moments, Kathy said, "Thank you. I'm all right. Please, do go on."

The doctor continued. "Because of the damage to James's heart, he is now at risk for congestive heart failure. His lungs are already compromised as well, so if he makes it out of the operating theatre alive, we're going to have to watch very closely for any heart or lung troubles. Because of all this hemorrhaging and the heart attacks, James's remaining kidney may have been ischemic at some point and he could still lose that one, too.

"James lost an awful lot of blood before the ambulance got to him and he didn't have a pulse or a heartbeat when they started working on him. We have no idea how long he was in that state. Because of that, along with the heart attacks and hemorrhaging, it may be that James's brain was anoxic, so there is the possibility of brain damage. With him being in a coma, we have no way of determining his neurological status until he wakes up. *If* he wakes up."

He paused to give the distraught mother a moment to begin to digest this terrifying information.

"There is some good news, though," he continued. "We took a look and did not find any perforations in his intestines or other internal organs, although it's still possible that we missed something. But we gave it as good a look as we could, and we think we repaired any existing damage.

"Also, James was really fortunate because one of the bullets just barely missed his spine. That could have been a devastating injury, had it been just the tiniest bit to one side. We've been filling him with blood, but it's been pouring out of him faster than we can replace it. Between that and the heart attacks...

"We've got him on loads of antibiotics, we're monitoring his heart continually, he's on a respirator, and as I said, we're keeping an eye on kidney function, and lots of other things. So he'll be in the ICU and hooked up to more tubes than you'll be able to count for a while."

Dr. Fortin was quiet for a moment, giving James's devastated mother and younger brother a chance to absorb all the information that had just been given to them. Then, looking Kathy directly in the face again, he said, "I have to be honest with you; we really don't expect him to survive the operation, never mind the night, and I'm sorry to have to tell you that. But you should know so that you can be prepared, and if he makes it to recovery, you can say whatever you need to say while you still have time. Patients report having been able to hear while they were in a coma, so James will know you are there. I think you should know that not long before I left the room, we had decided to call it quits. He's just taking too long to respond now to any stimulation to get his heart going again. In fact, they may have given up by now. A body can only withstand so much."

The doctor put his hand on Kathy's shoulder. "I'm so sorry, Mrs. Lane. If there's anything we can do for you or your family, I trust you will let us know. I'll send someone to take you to your son as soon as he's out of surgery. It shouldn't be long now; they were just preparing to close up his wounds when I left."

Kathy sat in stunned silence for a moment after he left her before turning and hugging Elijah. "Oh, Mummy! Did I really hear that correctly? They don't expect James to live? We have to go and say goodbye?" The boy was incredulous. Huge tears welled up in his big, beautiful eyes and quietly rolled down his cheeks. He simply could not believe what his family had been put through in the past year, and with this on top of it, he was feeling as though they were living in the middle of a very bad movie. It was just unthinkable that one family should have to endure so much.

"Yes, Elijah, you heard him correctly." Kathy fought to keep from falling apart as she took a deep breath and continued. "We need to find your father. Can you stay in the waiting room by yourself? One of us should be there in case he shows up, or if they come and tell us that we can go and see James."

"Sure, Mum. I'll stay. But please hurry back!"

"Of course I will, Son. Don't worry. I'll be as quick as I can."

Kathy was not familiar with this hospital, so she was not sure where to begin to search for her husband. She began by going to the emergency area but did not see him speaking with anyone there. She checked a couple of corridors between there and the waiting room, and decided to get drinks for herself and Elijah before heading back to her son. Hoping to find a vending machine, she checked her purse for change while she walked. But before she found a machine, she found the cafeteria.

Robert and Rosa had found a table so that Robert could 'decompress' a little before he had to go back and face Kathy. After about 15 minutes, Robert thanked Rosa for her support, and said he really needed to get going. He had left Kathy and Elijah for much longer than he had anticipated, having fallen apart for a while. He reached across the table and took one of Rosa's hands in both of his. He kissed it gently, then briefly laid his cheek against it, and stood up to leave.

As he walked toward the exit, he did not notice his wife standing near the entrance, with a clear view of the table where he had been sitting with Rosa.

Sixteen

It was nearly the middle of December. It had been a fortnight since James had been shot and miraculously, had survived. The doctors certainly had their work cut out for them when he arrived at the hospital, and there were many terrifying points in the days following, but everyone kept saying it must not have been his turn.

James lay in his bed recovering from the shooting. He had clear memories of drifting up to the bright light, and seeing Angelina, his grandparents, Billy and others who had died. It had seemed that he was floating heavenward for a long time, the light becoming brighter and warmer as he grew nearer, and finally, just when he began to go through the brightest part, where everyone was there with outstretched arms to welcome him, he was suddenly yanked back downward. He was back in his body, with tubes and machines hooked up everywhere. He had to wonder if it was just the drugs and the shock of being shot; he was afraid to say anything to anyone, certain that everyone would think he had lost the plot. He had heard Elijah talk a little about this stuff but he just thought it was nonsense. He struggled to believe that it was true, even after this experience.

One thing was for sure, though, if he had not been hallucinating, if the after life that he was certain he had seen was real, then dying wasn't so bad after all. It had been a beautiful feeling, so completely peaceful. He had known that he was dying and it was perfectly okay with him. He felt no fear; only the most incredible peace and tranquility. He could not believe how wonderful it had felt, floating into that beautiful light. And it was so good to see Angelina again, even if he only imagined it. He had tried so hard for so long to block her out of his memory, escaping her sweet face and almost all thoughts of her by using drugs and alcohol, it was like a the most wonderful homecoming, seeing her again. Recalling this, a few tears escaped the young man's eyes, and he quickly wiped them away.

It must have been the drugs they gave him when he was having the surgery. He had heard that those things can really knock you for a loop. Well, even if it was just a dream, it was a nice one for a change.

His life was sure in a mess, and he had no idea how he was going to fix it. Of course, the police were on him now, wanting to know all about how and why he was shot. He was still hoping that his drug dealing would not be discovered, and at this point, the police still assumed that he and Billy were simply mugged. But the police were pretty nosy, and he knew they were smart enough to figure out the truth. He was probably gonna have to come clean at some point, but for now, he was just biding his time, and wishing this would all go away.

It was pretty likely that Rider was the one who had shot him and Billy, and since no one mentioned finding any drugs on either of them, he could only assume that Rider had stolen them, along with any money they'd had.

Mike and Bull had been by to visit, along with Crazy, Mad Dog, and a few of the others. They never stayed long; James was just too weak and too tired, but they popped in to say hi and checked on their friend. They all felt pretty awful about what had happened to James and Billy, and some of them felt responsible, like they should have protected the boys, not let them get into that business, especially not when they were so young.

James reminded them of his temper and how he had been determined to do whatever he was going to do, and no one was going to stop him. He said that he was still pretty messed up, and that he had a lot to work out, but he didn't know exactly what that meant. One thing was certain, though: he wasn't going to let his friends take responsibility for the choices that he had made that had landed him in this position.

When he was alone, he allowed himself to cry about Billy, and he was very fearful that Rider might come back and try to finish off the job he started, in an effort to prevent James from identifying him as the likely suspect. He didn't want to share his weaknesses with anyone; he kept his fear and his tears to himself. He missed Billy something fierce. They had been best friends for as long as James could remember. He could not believe that he would never see his buddy again.

He wished that he could be more like Elijah; that kid really believed all that life-after-death and spiritual stuff. He seemed to be so accepting of things; was he right to do that? Or was he just in denial? Part of him wanted to talk to his little brother about everything in the past year, especially that experience or dream where he thought maybe he had actually gone and seen Angelina. But at least for now, he decided to keep all of this to himself. He was still in a lot of pain, still on a lot of medication, and he wasn't so sure that his brain was fully functional.

Plus the docs had talked about brain damage, so maybe he just went a little nuts and that's all it was that was causing the 'bright light memory'. Whatever it was, it would stay with him for now, and maybe forever. He had a lot of healing to do and he needed his energy to help him recover fully.

Kathy and Robert were, of course, greatly relieved after every life-threatening crisis passed and James managed to pull through again and again. It had to have been especially awful for Robert, being a doctor and knowing absolutely everything that could go wrong, given James's particular situation.

With the extent of James's injuries and the threat of his death looming for some time afterward, Kathy had decided to bite her tongue about what she had seen in the cafeteria. Watching Robert hold that woman's hand, then kiss it and hold it against his cheek in such a loving fashion was terribly painful, especially when she was seeing it immediately after having received such dreadful news about their son.

But Kathy managed to remember that she had a part in whatever might be going on between her husband and this very beautiful woman, and she also knew that she should not jump to conclusions, although it was clear that the woman held an important place in her husband's heart.

It just wasn't the time or the place, and all she could do at that time was keep it to herself, and wait until James was at least sorted before tackling any more big issues. Heaven knew they had more than enough of those already.

It was a terrible time for the couple, of course, wondering whether they were going to lose another of their children, and with Christmas approaching, they were reliving the horror of the previous year. Neither of them wanted anything to do with the holiday, not this year. And James still wasn't entirely out of the woods, so they weren't too keen on planning a celebration, only to have another child die in the middle of it.

They had so many issues between them, going back to the time of the accident; neither of them was fully aware of the extent of the problems yet, but they were both beginning to understand that there were many that needed resolution.

James was going to need a lot of care and time to heal, and although his chances of survival were increasing daily, they were not yet going to assume he would be well. His heart had suffered a lot of damage, and they knew that it created an ongoing threat to his survival. And on top of his physical injuries, he needed a lot of emotional help and support, but his parents were uncertain about whether or not he would be willing to accept it.

First things first; they had to make sure he recovered physically and could get home.

Elijah spent a lot of time at the hospital as well, although his parents thought he should be home with his Aunt Sandra, who had come to help out for a while. But he really wanted to be with his brother; he had seen so little of him throughout the year, knowing that although James didn't see it, he needed his family. So as far as Elijah was concerned, now that James was stuck in a bed, he was darned well going to get lots of family visits, whether he liked it or not.

So Sandra spent a fair bit of time at the hospital with everyone else, but Elijah was pushed to go back home with her, earlier than his parents were leaving. He still needed proper meals and rest, and it was time that he let others take care of him for a change.

One night, just a few days before Christmas, Elijah had that same dream again, the one he'd had a couple of times before James was shot, the one in which Angelina was telling him to make sure that the family celebrated the holiday. In this dream, she was even more insistent than in the others.

That day, Elijah thought it was time to ask his family about it. All of them were still in such a mess; his mother was forced out of living in her bedroom by the impending death of another child, so Elijah knew that just because she was up and around was by no means a sign that she was well. She looked haggard and gaunt, and she barely ate. Robert and Sandra kept trying to push food at her, but she picked at it, saying she was simply unable to eat.

Elijah was worried about his family's response to the idea of celebrating Christmas, but he continued to have this dream, and he was certain that it was Angelina trying to get this message to his family. Therefore, he believed that he had no choice but to do something about it, whether or not it upset anyone. It seemed that he had been protecting them forever. Maybe that had not been such a good idea. But whether or not that was true, it was time to stop.

That night, his Aunt Sandra had sent him to bed, knowing it was already past his bedtime, but she was good that way. She didn't worry so much about the rules when things were difficult, especially because she knew that Elijah wouldn't take advantage of her kind nature.

Elijah was planning to wait until his parents got home, and then speak to his dad about Christmas. For a long list of reasons, he did not believe that his mother could cope with the conversation.

Earlier that day, he had been contemplating whether to do it that night, or in the morning, or at the hospital tomorrow, or tomorrow night, but then he was right back to thinking he might as well just get on with it and do it as soon as possible. All their days were the same anyway; his parents were gone early and home late. There simply was not going to be a good time to ask them about this. And he was running out of time.

Kathy and Robert stayed at the hospital later than usual on that particular day, and Elijah was just about falling asleep when he finally heard their car drive up. His parents visited for a few minutes with Sandra, but then he heard them saying goodnight and climbing the stairs to their room.

Elijah took a deep breath and opened his door. After greetings among the three, Elijah summoned the courage to say what he knew needed to be said. "Dad? Can I talk to you for a minute, please?"

"Of course, Elijah. What's up?" Robert asked, as he followed the boy into his bedroom.

The two sat on his bed and the boy was silent for a moment, uncertain about how to begin this conversation.

Finally, Elijah heaved a large sigh and said, "I've been thinking. I don't think anyone in the family is too interested in having Christmas, but I think we should do it."

Silence.

Robert looked at the floor. Then he looked at Elijah, and opened his mouth as though he was about to say something. But he closed his mouth and stared at the floor once again. And still he said nothing.

After a minute or two, the man spoke, his tone soft and gentle. "Son, I don't think we can do it. Not this year," said Robert, apologetically. "We're in a huge mess. James is still so sick, and we already have the horrible memory of Angelina dying last Christmas. To be honest, I'm terrified that if we celebrate it and James dies, too, we just won't be able to cope with enduring this season forever after. We're struggling to keep ourselves collected, to be strong for James, never mind the rest of us."

Elijah's face fell. He looked positively crushed. Although this was the response he expected, it was not the one for which he had been hoping. "But Dad --"

Robert's hand went up, gesturing for the boy to be quiet. "I've thought a lot about this, and there is just no way that I can imagine us having anything to do with celebrating Christmas this year. Your mother is still a long way from well; I have serious concerns about how she has handled Angelina's death and I'm not sure what to do. But I really think celebrating Christmas will push her over the edge. And on top of that, it's only three days from now. Even if we thought we could emotionally handle it, we have no time to prepare now."

It broke Robert's heart to see the overwhelming disappointment on his young son's face. With so many people in this family having opposing emotional needs, he was at a loss as to how to cope with them at once. Someone was always going to be upset, no matter what decision was made.

"I'm sorry, Elijah. I know this has been an absolutely horrible year for you, but please, try to understand that this is just asking way too much of us. It would have been bad enough without James having been shot; we didn't want to celebrate Christmas anyway. But with your mother's precarious state, I really think that the best way for us to get through the first one without Angelina is just to let it pass.

"There has been too much for us to cope with, and now that James has been shot, and his heart is very weak -- well, I'm sorry, Elijah, but it just can't happen this year. I hope you can try to understand." Robert reached over and put his hand on the boy's arm.

Elijah was quiet. He was so disappointed. He knew that the dream was a message from Angelina, but he dared not say it, especially since his parents had enough problems hearing about anything to do with her. To tell them that she was behind this, that she was the one who was pushing for the celebration -- well, he was certain that it would not go over well.

His father kissed him goodnight and tucked him in. Turning out the light and shutting the door behind him, the heavy-hearted father went to bed.

Elijah had a brief chat with Angelina. He was pretty sure that she had listened in on the one he had just had with his father, since she had been urging him to do this. Certainly, he agreed that it was necessary for the family to celebrate, but he would not have had the courage to push for such a thing to happen, if not for Angelina coming to him in the dreams. He apologized to her, telling her that he had done his best, but it was clear that he should not mention it again. He hoped that James would get better, and the family could fix everything, and then maybe by next year, they would be ready to have Christmas again.

Elijah told her that he hoped she understood. And he added that he surely didn't.

Telling his sister goodnight, he turned over and after a few tears and a long time, finally drifted into an uneasy sleep.

Robert found Kathy already in bed when he entered their room. He was certain that she was not asleep; after all, he had not been with Elijah for more than just a few minutes. Yet she said nothing when he whispered to her, asking if she was still awake.

Her behaviour had been rather peculiar in the past several weeks, beginning with that morning he had got up and found her in the kitchen with a pot of coffee made. At times, it had almost seemed as though she was trying to take a few tiny hesitant steps back toward him, but then she retreated into her silence, into being alone, cutting herself off once again.

And since James was shot, the alternating moods seemed even more pronounced. On some occasions, Robert could almost see his wife again, the way she used to be, but then there was this dramatic retreating.

There was something else bothering him, too. Every now and then, he could hear Kathy quietly talking to herself, or at least, it seemed to be to herself. But once in a while, he thought he had heard a snippet or two, and he was certain that she was talking to Angelina, but not as though she realized that the girl was dead. Robert believed that Kathy was pretending that their Little Angel was still alive. He could not prove it, and he was quite certain that if he were to ask her, she would deny it.

While Robert brushed his teeth and got ready for bed, he began to formulate a plan which he hoped was going to help Kathy. He was certain that Sandra would be willing to assist because he had spoken with his sister about the situation with Kathy on many occasions. She, too, was very worried about it, and with any luck, what he had in mind may just work. But it certainly wasn't going to be pleasant.

Robert turned off the bathroom light and quietly crept into bed. His mind was rolling with thoughts of all the troubles in his family. Although there had not yet been any proof about it, the speculation was that James had been involved in drugs in a much bigger way than his father could have guessed. Elijah had been carrying the weight of the world on his little shoulders all year. And of course, Robert was deeply concerned about his wife's mental health, and was also uncertain about whether or not they could repair their marriage, even though he believed they still loved each other very much... which brought him to thoughts of Rosa.

Everything with her had been so simple before James was shot. When he could keep that part of his life as a sweet little fantasy, a bit of light and fun and relief from the burdens, the guilt, the oppression of too much grief, then it was beautiful and it was so easy.

But right from the moment that Kathy had called him to tell him that James was shot, and reality had come flooding into his perfect fantasy life with Rosa, everything had changed, and the fantasy had become very complicated. And that was because the fantasy no longer existed, not with that much reality. That night, the fantasy became the reality of two people who truly cared about each other, perhaps even loved each other, or maybe they were just 'in love' with each other. And these two people had separate lives that would not accommodate their feelings for each other, whether or not they offered some respite from the troubles of their lives, whether or not their time together contributed to their lives.

Up until that phone call, Robert and Rosa had been living with the illusion that their fantasy time together was not hurting anyone. Robert thought about how close they had come to crossing a line that would have changed everything on that fateful night. They fooled themselves and believed that since they were not engaging in a physical relationship, there was no harm in what they were doing. And even on that night, when they were prepared to cross that line, they still believed that they could continue to live in their fantasy world.

They could tell themselves that it wasn't a real relationship. In fact, they would never use that 'R' word in describing what they were sharing, and in this way, they reinforced the notion of this being a fantasy. And how could a fantasy, something 'not real' affect their lives outside of that?

It took the horror of James being shot for Robert to see just how destructive the fantasy could be. He had to realize that as long as Rosa was a real woman, then it was a real relationship, and there was no fantasy about it, simply because they had chosen to keep parts of their lives out of all conversation between them.

As much as Robert tried to convince himself that he could go back to his 'play time' with Rosa and not have it affect his life or his marriage, he knew that he was wrong. He was trying to find some justification, some rationale that would allow him to continue to see this beautiful, warm woman, with whom he had much in common, and in whose company he felt happy, peaceful and free.

Ah, denial is a wonderful thing. And it's a killer.

Robert had a choice to make. He could try to fix the disastrous mess that was his life and family, a task which seemed impossible, given that many of the problems were beyond his control, and could only be fixed if everyone else worked at them, too. Or he could leave the mess he had made and try to help clean it up from a distance, and include Rosa in his new life.

Neither choice was particularly appealing. Robert had not been looking to destroy what he had tried to build with Kathy, and most certainly, it was not in his plan when he met Rosa. He had simply been looking for some peace and some happiness. And he had taken the easiest route to find them, but it wasn't the best route. Nor was it going to bring him true peace or happiness, and the irony was that his fantasy happiness was going to cause very real pain.

Robert had taken a few steps back from his relationship with Rosa -- yes, he would have to call it that, whether he liked it or not -- after James was shot. He was on overload and had far too many serious things come crashing down around him at once. Nothing like a good, strong dose of reality to wake a person up. Even if he believed that he and Rosa could continue to see each other and simply call it a friendship, one which provided him with an ongoing source of strength, he finally understood that if he stopped running from so many of his own problems, he would have the strength he needed to cope with them. He understood that he was wasting a lot of energy on guilt, and most of all, on trying to ignore, or cover up numerous hurts and problems in himself, his marriage, his family.

It was time to stop wasting all that energy. It was time to take his head out of the sand. It was time to face reality. And whether or not his family liked it, whether or not it made them all want to leave him, things were going to change, effective immediately.

He was going to have to have The Talk with Rosa, and it broke his heart to think that he would never see or speak with her again, would never know how she was, what she was doing, what had become of her. But he knew they could never be ‘just friends’; he knew that their relationship had been very emotionally intimate, so much so that there was no going back, and enough to have created damage elsewhere. There was no choice but for them to say goodbye.

James was going to have to face reality, as well. He was going to have to come clean about his involvement with drugs, and about when, why and how that happened. This could mean some major altercations when those discussions were finally initiated, but Robert knew that it was time for everyone in the family to stop living in denial.

And the plan that he had for Kathy could go either way. It was going to be very painful, whatever the end result, but it was absolutely necessary.

He would discuss it with Sandra in the morning, or at least, at the first chance he had when Kathy was not present.

Robert’s head was spinning with a growing number of issues that were becoming clear to him, and he saw an increasing list of concerns that this family needed to address if it was ever going to be functional and healthy again. He lay awake for a long time that night, and finally, overcome with exhaustion, he fell into a deep sleep.

And just across the hall, Elijah was being visited again by Angelina while he slept.

Seventeen

The dawn brought with it a chilly wind and a lot of snow. The overcast sky matched the grey, fuzzy feeling in Robert's head after his very late night. He felt relieved about having discovered so many ways in which he thought his family could get back on the right track, but his stomach was also knotted up, and he was filled with apprehension when he contemplated all that had to happen between that moment and whatever outcome there might be. It was, to say the very least, extremely overwhelming just thinking about it, never mind expecting himself and his family to follow through and accomplish all of those changes.

One thing at a time, he told himself. The first order of the day was to talk to Sandra and see when they could arrange to carry out his plan to try to help Kathy. He got dressed and went downstairs to see if his sister was up and about yet, hoping that they could talk before his wife got out of bed.

Elijah heard his dad going downstairs, followed by the quiet tones of his voice and Aunt Sandra's. He was going to have to talk to his dad again; Angelina was being very insistent about celebrating Christmas, despite what their father had said the previous night. And it was December 23; there was not much time. He had butterflies in his tummy, afraid that he was going to upset his father, but Angelina was not taking no for an answer. And Elijah was really stuck between a rock and a very hard place.

Slowly, the lad got dressed and tried to figure out how and when he could put this to his father. He contemplated telling his dad the truth, the whole story about Angelina instigating these requests, but he always ended up at the same place. He wanted to protect his family from being hurt, so he thought he should leave that part out of the equation. Maybe they still needed protecting in some ways after all.

Once downstairs, Elijah found his dad, chatting with Aunt Sandra in the kitchen.

"Good morning, Elijah!" Aunt Sandra smiled at him.

"Morning, Son, how are you today?" asked his dad.

Elijah was quiet and stood at the doorway, biting his lower lip.

Aunt Sandra's smile changed to a look of concern. And so did Robert's. "What's the matter, Elijah?" he asked the boy.

Elijah stared at the floor for a moment and continued to bite his lip. No matter how hard he tried, he simply could not make the words come out this morning. Angelina was going to have to be patient. She was going to have to understand that this wasn't as easy for him as she might have thought.

"Nothing, Dad. I'm okay. Just tired." And after getting himself a glass of orange juice, he turned and left the room.

Sandra and Robert looked at each other. That boy was so deep; there was always something going on way down inside him, and most of the time, no one had any idea what it might be. He was always pondering something spiritual or philosophical, and seemed to spend his life having Big Things on his mind. For a kid, he sure didn't play much. They could understand why that had been the case over the past year, but even before that, he was more inclined to read books that were intended for readers well beyond his years, and even more often, he would just sit and contemplate the wonders of the Universe, or spiritual matters, or the meaning of life. He was a wise, old soul, and unfortunately, what little 'kid' there was in him was pretty much squashed after Angelina died.

It was another of those issues that Robert expected to disappear once things started to change in the family. The only trouble was, how could he get the ball rolling?

Well, at least he had a partial answer to that question. Sandra was going to help him with the first part, the one that he thought was the most pressing, the most immediately important. She was going to help him execute the plan he had for Kathy.

And she was going to help him today.

Robert, Elijah and Sandra were having breakfast when Kathy finally made an appearance. She looked pale and drained, and a good deal older than she actually was. She slumped into a chair at the kitchen table while Sandra poured a cup of coffee for her. Elijah finished eating, and put his dishes by the sink before going upstairs to get dressed.

An awkward silence hung in the air, but Kathy was not quite conscious enough to notice. Either that or she chose not to acknowledge it. But Robert and Sandra certainly felt it. They knew what was on the agenda for the day and they were rather nervous, anticipating all manner of unpleasantries.

Sandra finished her breakfast, and asked if she could get anything for her sister-in-law. Kathy said, "No, thanks very much, I've got my coffee," and although the others present were certain that she should try to eat something, they thought better of giving her any pressure today. Little did she know, it was about to become something of a nightmare for her. And unfortunately, there was no way to avoid it.

Robert helped clear away the breakfast things from the table while Sandra did the washing up. Kathy sat and drank her first cup of coffee, then got a refill before heading for the stairs.

"I'll just go and get ready for the hospital now," she called over her shoulder to the co-conspirators in the kitchen, who looked at each other and felt very guilty, although they knew they would be doing the right thing.

"Sure, Kath," answered Robert. "We're ready when you are." Although truth be told, he knew she would never be ready for what he had in mind.

He was pacing a bit, but trying to stop. He did not want to arouse any suspicion. Elijah came down and put on his boots and coat in the porch. "I'm going to wait outside, Dad," he said. Something felt really awful and anxious in the house, and he was being bombarded by that energy. He knew something was up, but he didn't know what. And it didn't seem like a very good 'something', the way he was feeling. Sometimes, he wished he were not so sensitive and intuitive. Sometimes, when there were unpleasant things going on around him, it felt like a physical assault. And this was one of those occasions.

It wasn't too long before the four were gathered, all dressed in appropriate winter wear. It was a very chilly morning, and every time the wind picked up, it was an extra little bite or sting that none of them particularly needed.

At least the car was warm, so it wasn't going to be too bad.

Except that two of the occupants in the car were unaware that there would be more exposure to the elements than they knew.

There was not much conversation as the car headed down the road and away from the cottage. Kathy thought it was just another day, beginning with a trip to the hospital to visit James, and because he was improving, there was talk of him coming home soon. She sat in the front passenger seat, staring out the window, contemplating the happy day when her son would be released, and hoping that nothing else went wrong to prevent it.

Robert and Sandra were thinking about The Plan, each filled with anticipation, dread, hope, fear.

Elijah sat in the back with his aunt, absorbing everything that was flying around him, questioning, apprehensive, anxious, feeling that something ominous was lurking.

It was not long before Kathy was startled out of her thoughts when she noticed that Robert had taken an unexpected turn. With a puzzled look, she turned to him and asked what he was doing.

"Just making a quick stop on our way to see James," Robert replied, his heart pounding in his chest as his plan was now set in motion.

Kathy had not been paying any attention to where Robert was going, so lost in thought was she. And although she noticed that they were going the wrong way, she did not immediately recognize this road.

As she stared out the window, the puzzled expression soon turned to one of surprise, and then to one of fear. And then, oh, my heaven, then it was one of rage.

Kathy began yelling at Robert, not caring that there were other people in the car, not caring that one of them was her young son. She said terrible, hurtful things to him as he drove through the cemetery gates. She was livid, and struggled to undo her seatbelt, saying she was getting out of the car, although it was still moving, albeit very slowly.

She was in tears, and was shaking uncontrollably. She lashed out at everyone in the car, saying that they were all in on it, even blaming Elijah for participating in this horrible thing, screaming at him that he should have warned her, should have stopped this, and she would never forgive him.

The boy sat in stunned silence during his mother's tirade. He could not believe that his father had brought her here, and he could not believe the words that were coming out of her mouth. But in thinking about it, he completely supported his father. He believed that this was exactly what his mother needed. She had never accepted Angelina's death, and until she did, the rest of this family could not begin to heal. If he was right about his mother pretending that her Little Angel was still alive, then that was even more reason for his father to do this.

And because he understood and supported this decision, he was prepared to take whatever his mother threw at him until she figured it out.

Robert kept driving while Kathy alternated between screaming at him in rage, and begging him through tears. Hurling accusations and insults did not stop him, nor did her pleading or her crying. Slowly, he made his way through the snow-covered cemetery, following the road to a place near Angelina's grave, at which point Robert pulled over and turned off the car.

Kathy screamed at Robert to start the engine and get going. She swore that she was not getting out, unless it was to walk home. She threatened to leave Robert altogether if he did not take her out of there immediately. She cried like a little girl, saying she really didn't want to be there and would he please, please, *please* take her home.

She tried just about everything she could think of. And Robert, Sandra and Elijah all just sat in silence while she got it all out of her system.

Many times, one or the other of them expected her to get out and start to tramp through the snow, and try to walk home, but surprisingly, she did not actually do it. She did not even open the car door. She just sat and ranted and raved, cried and screamed, yelled and raged until she was drained, exhausted, and thoroughly spent.

Finally, inside the car, it was absolutely silent, except for the sound of Kathy trying to catch her breath. Outside, there was only the occasional bird singing, or the sound of a distant car on the highway. The sun was breaking through the clouds, and the snow sparkled on the trees, the ground, the frost on the gravestones.

No one was moving. No one was speaking.

After a time, Elijah opened the door and got out. Opening his mother's door, he offered her a little mittened hand, gesturing for her to take it and step outside, but he did not say a word.

Kathy looked at her beautiful son, her eyes brimming with tears, her lip quivering as she fought fresh waves of sobs. And upon seeing his little mittened hand, while she sat there in the cemetery, just feet away from Angelina's grave, she recalled the horrible doctor's appointment about a year earlier. She remembered her daughter's sweet little mittened hand in hers, while they walked along the sidewalk full of Christmas shoppers. She remembered the Little Angel in the window, the one with the yellow hair, and the horror of thinking that Angelina would soon die.

There were floods of memories then, Angelina's last days, the good and wonderful moments, the heartbreaking ones when she was so visibly ill, the moment of her death.

Elijah had not moved, nor had Robert or Sandra. It seemed an eternity since her son had offered his little hand to her, but Kathy knew that it was probably only seconds. She knew he loved his mother; she knew she could trust her boy in his great wisdom.

Finally, hesitantly, Kathy put her gloved hand in his mittened one, and although her heart broke just a little in that moment, it began to heal with each step that she took with her son toward Angelina's grave.

Robert and Sandra got out of the car and followed several steps behind, catching up to Elijah and Kathy moments after they reached the beautiful tombstone that marked their sweet daughter's resting place.

Robert had been here months ago to see to the tombstone's placement. But otherwise, none of them had been to the cemetery since the funeral. Each had a personal reason for that choice. Robert felt too much guilt, and combined with his grief, he just could not face the pain that it would bring to sit and stare at the ground, knowing his daughter was buried several feet below.

James was mostly too angry with Angelina for having created so much heartbreak in the family, even long before she was born. It hurt him too much to think about how much he loved and missed his sweet little sister, so the young man did what most people do: he turned his pain into anger.

Kathy, of course, was far too overcome with grief, and then denial. She had put herself into a wonderful fantasy world, where Angelina still lived, still helped her bake, still talked to her, still needed her hair brushed, and stories read. She knew that seeing that grave would mean the end of her fantasy world. It would mean accepting that her daughter was dead. It would mean she would never see her Little Angel again.

Elijah would not have minded going to the cemetery, had anyone else been going, but he did not feel the need to attend because he knew that this is not where Angelina really was. It was just her body that was there, but her Spirit lived on, right there with them. Of that, he was certain, yet no one else in his family shared his beliefs.

Oh, if only they did! The past year would not have been so horrible and dark if only they knew that Angelina would live forever, and that she was still with them.

Well, at least his father had done something that might finally help his mother. Time would tell, but Elijah thought that maybe now, she would begin to accept the fact that Angelina was dead.

The four stood at the grave for a while. After a time, Kathy knelt down in the snow and touched the tombstone, using her gloved finger to trace the letters in Angelina's name, and the picture of the little angel that was beside it.

Finally, she whispered, "Goodbye, my Angel," and kissing two fingers, she then touched them to the tombstone and rose. After one last look, she turned and went back to the car without another word.

The others spent another moment or two at the grave, and also shared private thoughts with Angelina. And once they were all back in the car, they turned and headed for the hospital without looking back.

Eighteen

The next morning, Christmas Eve, Dr. Fortin said that James could go home for an overnight visit so he could spend Christmas with the family. No one had told him that there would be no celebration, and he assumed that like most patients, James would want to be with his family for those two days.

James didn't much care whether or not there was 'Christmas', with presents and turkey and all of that. He was just so happy to be out of the hospital for a while, that was all that mattered. Dr. Fortin had said that once he checked in again, if his tests continued to look okay for a day or two after having been up and around more normally, he would discharge him, knowing that the boy's father was a doctor and that he would be in good hands.

Sandra and Elijah spent the morning getting James's room ready for him, while Kathy and Robert went to collect their son. Elijah was very excited; it had been such a long time since they had been like 'normal brothers'. He knew that just having James in the house didn't fix everything, and he was not about to pretend that there were no problems. But he figured they had to start somewhere, and this was as good a place as any.

He was, however, feeling rather upset about Angelina's messages. She had come to him in a dream again the night before. She kept urging him to insist that the family celebrate Christmas, but after the past couple of days, he really did not dare. It was easy for her to expect him to pull this off, but she was in a whole different place where people didn't get angry or hurt like they did on Earth! And he just knew that it was the wrong time to bring it up again.

He had been pushed to make a choice. On the one hand, there was his sister, trying to push him to do something, something with which he agreed. But on the other hand, there was his father, telling him a flat out 'NO' with lots of good reasons, and there was the knowledge that if he pushed, Elijah could really upset his family.

Angelina had put him in a terrible position, and if anything, he should probably be annoyed with her for it! But he couldn't do that. He wasn't really annoyed. He just wished that she would stop pressuring him. It just wasn't going to happen this year, and she would have to be the one to understand.

Elijah was suddenly hit with an idea that he thought was brilliant! And in fact, maybe it was what Angelina wanted! There was no reason why the two of them couldn't acknowledge Christmas, just by themselves. No one else had to know! He could paint a Christmas tree and things like that, and they could have their own little party.

Yes! That's what he would do! The lad felt better, believing that he had found a good compromise which would appease his sister without hurting his family.

And after he had finished making a welcome card for James, he set to work creating some Christmas goodies for his little party with Angelina.

Because of the distance to the hospital and back, and the time it took to organize James's release, meds and other red tape, it took a few hours before the weak and exhausted young man was finally helped into his home by his parents.

Had he been alone, he probably would have cried at the sight of the place. It was wonderful to be back; he had not been there since the night he was shot. Part of him wanted to stay up and just 'be' in his house, and part of him was so drained and weak, he just had to go and rest. Remembering Dr. Fortin telling him that he must be very easy on himself, he took the advice he was given and went to lie down.

It felt so good to be back in his room, to see his guitars, his CDs, and to see his bed, where he used to see Angelina sitting and playing...

Lying in the hospital recovering for the past few weeks, James had been given a lot of opportunity to think about things. Despite the terrifying shooting, James still felt somewhat rebellious and defensive. Yes, of course he was aware that he should be thinking about making some huge changes, but he was ambivalent. Confused about his life, his family, his place in the world, not to mention the 'out of body experience' or dream that he had, he really had no idea where to start, never mind how to begin to try to put things together in a different way. People seemed to think that the shooting had to affect him in a way that would make him be squeaky clean, a goodie-two-shoes, and not only did this puzzle him, he knew that was certainly not going to happen. Sure, it changed him, but he was still trying to figure out just exactly what that meant.

For now, he just wanted to crawl into his bed and go to sleep. All he could handle was to take life one day at a time. Heck, a minute at a time. His life was in a million pieces, like a puzzle all over the floor, and there was no picture on a box to use for guidance, no way of knowing how the pieces were supposed to fit together, or how the picture should look when he was finished.

And how could he even think about finishing putting them together, when he hadn't a clue how to begin?

With a discouraged sigh, James pulled the duvet up over his body, and weak and exhausted from having just left the hospital, soon he fell fast asleep.

Kathy had been quiet for much of the time since she said goodbye to Angelina at the cemetery the previous day. She was too emotionally drained to have the energy to be upset or angry or anything else, really. A part of her felt a sense of peace and closure, but mostly, it just felt as though the wound was fresh and raw, as if the grief was new, as if her daughter had just died. And it did not help that the trip to the cemetery was two days before the anniversary of Angelina's death.

She desperately wanted to hide in her bedroom again, but Sandra encouraged her to resist the feeling as much as possible, at least while James was home. Gently, her sister-in-law tried to help her see that hiding was not going to change anything. Somehow, someday, she was still going to have to get used to living without Angelina. She may never really come to terms with what happened to her daughter, but she had to learn to live with it.

And she had been trying to get used to living with the image of Robert with that woman at the hospital on the night that James was shot. She wondered whether that was Rosa, and she had been chewing on it ever since.

There had simply not been a good time to discuss it, with everything else that this family was enduring.

Besides, if Robert had been having an affair, she had to admit that she pushed him into it. If she'd had any doubts about that before, the trip to the cemetery certainly opened her eyes and she could see much more clearly than before that their lives were in shambles, and if he had needed to turn to someone else during the worst time of his life, it was because she had refused to be there for him, caught up in her own selfish needs and pain.

For now, she was content to say nothing and just see how things went for them. If there was another woman, she was going to have a fight on her hands, even if neither Robert nor his mistress was ever aware of it, and he would eventually be pushed to the point of having to make a decision. Meanwhile, Kathy just knew that it was not time to bring up the possibility. She knew it was best to leave it alone.

It was Christmas Eve, but it certainly did not feel like it to anyone in the Lane home that day. Robert had gone to the woods to get some logs for the fire. Kathy was playing a game of

Uno with Elijah. Sandra was making dinner and James had been having his nap after arriving home at mid-day.

Being late afternoon in December, the sun was beginning to set and it would soon be dark. Kathy put down the cards long enough to light a fire.

"It's getting a bit chilly in here, isn't it, Elijah?" she asked. "How about asking Aunt Sandra if she'll make some hot chocolate for everyone?"

"Sure, Mum," replied Elijah, and as he headed for the kitchen, James came down the stairs, yawning and gingerly stretching, so as not to cause himself any pain.

"Hey, James," said Elijah. "You want some hot chocolate?"

"Sure, thanks," and James actually smiled at the prospect, thinking how that was not the kind of drink that made him happy most of the time, but it sure sounded good just then.

Elijah had delivered the message to Aunt Sandra, who immediately busied herself filling a heavy pot with milk and getting to work making the hot chocolate. The boy returned to the sitting room, where his mother and brother were keeping warm by the fire.

Kathy picked up the deck of Uno cards. "Another hand?" she asked Elijah.

"Okay! James, you wanna play with us?"

Before James could answer, there was a peculiar sound on the porch at the same time as they heard a sharp knock.

Kathy went to the door, a look of concern on her face, wondering what was the cause of the strange sound. Opening the door, she and the boys were astonished to see Robert standing there with a tree that he had apparently cut down from their woods and dragged home on his own.

Elijah was elated! He could not stop jumping up and down and squealing. James and Kathy were unable to speak, and Sandra came wandering in from the kitchen, wiping her hands on her apron, asking what all the noise was about. Upon seeing Robert dragging in the Christmas tree, she could not help but smile.

After getting over the shock, both James and Kathy had to admit to themselves that they felt some excitement about the tree, although Kathy did have to excuse herself at one point and go and have a quiet little cry on her own. But the good thing was that she didn't stay away long; she returned to her family, and smiled as she asked Elijah to go to the cellar and collect all the decorations and lights.

It was going to be a very bitter-sweet event; the family was remembering wonderful Christmases past, as well as the tragic one from last year. They were remembering all of Angelina's trips to Father Christmas, plus the ones the boys had when they were little. They heard the echos of laughter and happy chatter while wrapping paper was shredded and thrown around the room in the excitement of gift opening. And all of them had mixed feelings about letting go of the past, about facing, never mind embracing the future.

Elijah was busy carrying up boxes of decorations and lights, one of the first boxes being the one which contained the tree stand so that Robert could get started.

Just as they had done on their last tree-decorating evening, and all others before in this family, all the sitting room lights were dimmed, and the room was mostly lit by the fire and many candles. James got very brave and put on the family's favourite CD of Christmas carols. He was still not certain about all of this, or about anything else, and he did not dive in as much as he might have done, but there was a lot going on for the lad. He sat back and watched the others, occasionally contributing an idea, but mostly, just feeling like all he could do was stick his toe in the water.

When Sandra brought in the steaming hot chocolate in mugs and passed them around, she sat next to James. She contemplated throwing an arm around him, but it did not feel like he would appreciate that just yet. It was apparent that the boy still had a lot of wounds to heal, but she was confident that in time, it would happen. How much time, no one could guess, and it could be a very rocky road for him in the meantime. But she believed that someday, even if it was a long time in the future, someday, he would be okay.

Although no one present acknowledged it out loud, it was wonderful to hear the Christmas carols again. Now and then, someone or another would start humming or singing a little, and then, as if it was a bad idea, would abruptly stop. Clearly, they were struggling with the idea of celebrating or being happy with the Angelina's death so obviously in their minds.

The tree was looking beautiful as lights, Victorian ornaments and garlands were added. The room was looking rather festive as well, with pretty decorations hung on the walls, the mantle, or standing on table tops.

The decorating was nearly complete when there was another knock at the door. Everyone looked at the others, and there were comments about not expecting anyone, and maybe it was some neighbours coming for a little eggnog.

James went to the door and opened it; however, no one was there but the gently falling snowflakes. He had a good look, called "Hello!" a couple of times, but no one answered. Just as he was about to close the door, he noticed a box, beautifully gift-wrapped, sitting on the porch. And oddly, there were no footprints in the freshly fallen snow.

He picked up the pretty box with the brightly coloured paper and ribbons, with a big, red bow on top, and closed the door.

"Who is it from?" the question was uttered by everyone present.

"I don't know," replied James. "There's no card."

"Open it!" cried Elijah. "Maybe it will tell us inside!"

James very carefully undid the bow and ribbons, and peeled off the beautiful paper. There was an old box inside, with tattered edges and corners. With both hands, James gently lifted the lid while his family waited with great anticipation.

"Silent Night" began to play on the stereo. It was the song that was playing when Angelina put the angel on the tree for her first -- and only -- time. As the young man reached inside the box and removed its contents, his eyes grew wide and his mouth fell open. There, in the warmth of their dimly lit sitting room, was their beautiful antique angel, unbroken except for the chip on her left wing.

No one said a word for some time.

Finally, it was Robert who was able to speak. "How on earth..."

Elijah answered, "Earth has nothing to do with it, Dad."

Everyone was still standing and staring at the angel, and especially at the chip on the wing, listening to the last verse of "Silent Night". There was not a dry eye in the room.

Kathy spoke up. With tears in her eyes and a lump in her throat, she asked, "Elijah, as the youngest child, are you ready to put the angel on the tree and make a wish?" It was a question that held more meaning than an outsider would never possibly imagine. By referring to Elijah as the youngest child, the grieving mother was finally acknowledging that Angelina was dead. Everyone present knew that this family was about to begin their healing journey.

Elijah did not need to be asked twice. Robert lifted him up so that he could affix the angel to the top of the tree, and then set him back down again. The family heard the next song on the CD begin, "O Holy Night", and again, they remembered Angelina making her wish as it played the previous year.

"Your wish, Elijah. What is it?" asked Aunt Sandra, filled with anticipation.

Elijah looked up at the beautiful angel, perched atop the Christmas tree, and he paused for a moment, listening to the words to the song. "A thrill of hope, the weary world rejoices, for yonder breaks a new and glorious morn."

Elijah closed his eyes and with as much feeling as a person could possibly put into words, he said, "I wish I could have my family back."

And as tears streamed down faces, and lumps grew in throats, the dim lights went out completely, leaving the room lit only by candles. A little breeze came out of nowhere and whistled through the room, causing all the candles to flicker. It was felt by everyone and sent shivers up the spines of all who were present. The carol continued, "O night Divine..."

Just then, a swirling light filled the room, circling the tree several times until it reached the top where it hovered. No one could move and all were speechless. Staring up at the radiant light which grew brighter each moment, they were astonished when suddenly, there appeared their Little Angel, her beautiful dark curls framing her delicate face and rosy cheeks, looking perfectly happy and healthy in her white dress with the gold embroidery, and her feathery white wings, just like the angel that she and her mother had seen a year earlier, except her hair wasn't yellow.

"Hello, my family! Oh, this is so much fun! Elijah, my sweet brother, you wished to have your family back, and here we are, all together again. But you have been right all along! You have been saying that I've been here with all of you, and it is true. We have never really been apart, except for the emotional distance that you have put between yourselves and each other."

There were several pair of wide eyes on the faces of those present as the Little Angel continued. "I have been watching you since I left. And I have so much to tell you, but I am not allowed much time with you.

"First, you have all been missing me, wishing that I could still be with you in the physical world. I know that's because you were sad and just wanted to be with me. But think about this: Look at what happened to you! Look at how much time you wasted when you had other people right here in the same house, people who meant as much to you as I do, yet you have all been off by yourselves, wasting precious time that you could have been -- and should have been -- together! You were still a family, even without me being here the way I used to be!

"And you were choosing to grieve alone, rather than share your pain with others who missed me just the same. Mama and Daddy, I thought you taught us to share our troubles, but nobody did that after I left, and it made everything so much worse!"

Everyone had to agree that so far, she was entirely correct.

"You were all willing to throw away your happiness and ignore your relationships because you loved and missed me. That didn't make any sense to me at all! How could you be honouring your memories of loving me by destroying what you had with each other?

"And besides, I was with you very often, but you couldn't see, hear or feel me most of the time. I tried so hard to communicate with all of you, and sometimes it worked a little. But mostly, it didn't because you were not as open to receiving my messages as you needed to be. This was because you were too caught up in your grief, in missing me. You thought of me as being gone and were not open to believing that I was right here. All of you, that is, except Elijah. He was the most open. We spent lots of time together in my room, and sometimes other places, and I even went to him in dreams. He didn't tell you that, but I've been after him to encourage you to celebrate Christmas. He was afraid that telling you about the dreams would upset you. Elijah has spent too much time protecting the family, and putting his own needs and feelings aside."

All present had to agree, but it was Kathy who spoke. "Yes, my Angel, you are so right. I've been seeing it lately, and I'm now trying to sort out what I need to do to put things right. And I'm so sorry about my many mistakes."

"We all know you are, Mama. It was really awful for you when I left. You did your best. But now it's time to do things differently. It's not good to pretend that I'm still alive. You were afraid that if you believed I was dead, I would disappear from your life and your memory completely, and you were afraid that I would be hurt somehow. First of all, it's only my physical body that is dead, but that is not me, and I will always be here, just in a different way.

"And secondly, the only way you have hurt me is by not going on with life after I left. I know you will never forget me, Mummy, but it's time for you to live again. I'm still here. I sit on your lap and I touch your hair and I cuddle up with you lots. Sometimes you think I'm there, but then you're afraid you're imagining it. But you're not.

You must stop grieving for my death, and remember my life, and know that I am still here with you. I was very happy yesterday, Mummy, when you said goodbye to me at my grave. Yes, I was there, too. I'm with you more than you will ever know."

Kathy stood in silence, tears streaming down her face, overwhelmed with love for her daughter, and gratitude for the ability to hear these words.

"Daddy, you feel guilty for things that are not your fault. And you're afraid to say things that need saying. That has made you very sick in your heart. You have been hurting when you did not need to! You always do your best, and sometimes you try too hard to make everybody happy, but it makes you sad. There's not much point in that, is there? Silly Daddy!" Angelina giggled, her sparkling little girl laugh had not changed.

"No, my Little Angel, there isn't. You're right. My goodness, but you've learned many things, haven't you?" Robert said.

"Yes, Daddy. And there's something else. Mummy was pretending that I was still alive, and that made her happy in a pretend way. You were really worried about her for doing that, but there are lots of ways for us to pretend to be happy, but none of them will work. It's best to remember what's real because otherwise, it's like living in a big lie. And you always said lying was really bad, Daddy."

Robert was stunned and he had absolutely no response for her, except to hang his head and choke back a wave of sobs. Both of them knew exactly what she meant. And Kathy suspected that she did, too.

Angelina continued. "And I've been watching you, too, James. And you almost came to be with me. You smiled at me then, as you were coming through the bright light where I was waiting for you."

James was astonished! It had been true! He really had seen her! Everything Elijah said about an after-life was, indeed, the truth!

Angelina continued, "Oh, James, you are so angry! You are eating yourself up! If you saw how much it hurt the family when I left, how could you do the same thing to them? You took yourself away, you wouldn't talk to anyone, you started to do things to destroy yourself! How do you think that would have helped, if you had ended up with me?"

"Oh, Angelina. I never thought of it like that!" replied the young man, struggling to believe any of this. "I was just so angry because you died and everything fell apart after that. And I missed you so! I missed having you sit on my bed while I practiced. I missed reading to you. I missed playing Pooh Sticks!" James suddenly felt like a lost little boy. He was in tears, no longer caring if anyone knew how much he hurt.

"Ah, Pooh Sticks! Do you remember in Billy's car last winter?" Angelina queried.

James was silent for a moment as he tried to figure out what she was talking about. Suddenly, the memory came to him. It was the first time he had gone to Mad Dog's, and for some reason, just out of the blue, he had started thinking about Pooh Sticks on the way home.

His eyes widened. "Was that you?" he asked her, incredulous.

"Yes! I wanted you to know that I was still with you, and to let you know how special and important you always made me feel!" she giggled again.

"It took my physical death to bring all of you to the point of needing to fix things that have been wrong for a long time. You all stopped living long before I was even born. I watched you do it before I joined you in the physical world, and part of my purpose in this family was to teach you about this.

"Mummy and Daddy, you got so hung up on having more babies that you could not just accept and be grateful for the two that you had. You really needed to appreciate the blessings that you already had, and the really big one, the one where you and Elijah did not die in that terrible accident.

"Just think! It could have just been James and Daddy after that! But you didn't think of that. All you thought about was what you didn't have, instead of the beautiful blessings of life and love that you had already been given.

"And then when you lost me, all of you ended up alone! I know Elijah didn't want it to be that way; he has been trying to help all of you; he had so much to offer, but none of you listened. And as wise as he is, he's still just a child, so he just wasn't able to make the right things happen.

But James, Mummy and Daddy, you all buried yourselves and hid in different ways.

"I've been very sad for all of you, watching you wasting so much time when you could have been loving and supporting each other, remembering the good days we had together, and making more happy memories with each other. Do you not remember how you all pulled together to make it a wonderful Christmas season for me last year? Why have you not done this for each other? You have all needed it as much as I did!"

Everyone was dumbfounded by the wisdom and lessons that they were learning from their Little Angel.

"You already had your wish Elijah. You already had your family, and I have still been here, too. I was there on your first day back at school. I saw you change the calendar. I've heard you talking to me in lots of places. We are all still together, and we are all still a family. You just won't be able to see me like before. And besides, a family doesn't always have to be together in order to be a family! Think about how many people move far away from each other, but that doesn't stop them from loving each other!

"Your family let you down, Elijah, but that's okay. Everybody has to learn lessons, and you've all had plenty of those this year. Now it's time for me to leave, but remember that I'm still here and I'll always be part of your lives. Love and family do not end with distance or with death."

And with that, Angelina's image began to fade as the light around her grew brighter once again, swirling around the tree several times. Kathy, Robert, Sandra and the boys called goodbye to Angelina, and they blew kisses and wept as the swirling light faded with her image until both had vanished.

No one could speak for several minutes. They stood staring at the space above the tree where Angelina had been just moments before, Christmas carols still playing in the background.

This family had endured many terrible hardships for a long time and finally, they had real hope that they were going to be just fine. They had learned some very painful but valuable lessons, and had found themselves lost and struggling, feeling completely alone and lacking in any direction or stability.

Everything they needed had been right there all along; they had love and they had each other, and they had Elijah's wisdom to add a much needed spiritual element to their lives.

Loving relationships and spirituality are the foundation for celebrating Christmas at all. The previous year, the family had struggled to find any Christmas spirit when they knew Angelina was going to die, focusing on what they were losing, rather than on the blessings they had. And how ironic it was that the Christmas Spirit which brought them help and healing a year later was the Little Angel herself.

Yes, it was, indeed, a night Divine.

About Rikki

To say that Rikki is quirky is something of an understatement. Her favourite expression is that she lives so far outside the box, she can't see it any more. Some of her very favourite things are old doors, creaky things, bare feet, the moon, old stuff that's falling apart, and creating conversations in silly voices for animals, insects, and anybody else she happens to find in nature.

She finds the greatest of pleasures in some of the simplest of things, like giggling, bad puns, red peppers, misty days, listening to a howling wind, covering her living room ceiling in years' worth of her children's art work, and listening to her very favourite music played loudly enough to burst the neighbour's eardrums.

Rikki's first book, "The Spirit Within", has been extremely well-received as a work that provides comfort, healing and hope to many (www.booksbyrikki.com).

Her second book, "Animal Pen Pals", offers an unusual and highly entertaining view of life, relationships, the world, making readers of all ages laugh out loud, and cry quiet tears of sadness as they relate to the heartbreak of missing loved ones through moving away, or through death. (www.animalpenpals.com). It is filled with a wide range of lessons, values, emotions and experiences, and no doubt you will find the characters endearing and the stories heartwarming, whether you are 8 or 80.

Currently, Rikki resides in a quaint 1700s stone cottage that is about as quirky as she is. It is located in a tiny village in England, a couple of minutes' walk from a lovely little lake. In her life, she has loved walking, cooking, target shooting, gardening, travel, painting (www.artbyrivkah.com), sketching, decorating, and numerous other activities. She values respect, responsibility and honesty, and she is passionate about every moment of this Life.

Printed in the United Kingdom
by Lightning Source UK Ltd.
106656UKS00001B/106-153

9 781420 885484